# THE
# OTHER SIDE
# OF COMO

T0160145

First published in 2018
by Eyewear Publishing Ltd
Suite 333, 19-21 Crawford Street
London, W1H 1PJ
United Kingdom

*Cover design and typeset by* Edwin Smet
*Printed in England by* TJ International Ltd, Padstow, Cornwall

ISBN 978-1-912477-63-0

FIAT La nuova Balilla – per tutti, eleganza della Signora.
The new Fiat Balilla, Dudovich, Marcello (1878-1962).
Credit: De Agostini Picture Library/Bridgeman Images.

Pagani's Restaurant, Great Portland St (T138) with thanks to Westminster City Archives.
Ruskin Window, St Giles' Church, Camberwell Green, with thanks to St Giles Church.

*This book is a fictional account of a true story
and real historical events, drawn from a variety of sources, including
published materials and actual locations. No resemblance to persons living
or dead should be inferred, as characters are either the product of the author's
imagination or are used fictitiously.*

WWW.EYEWEARPUBLISHING.COM

# THE OTHER SIDE OF COMO

## MARA G. FOX

*'... mi se sperde a'l vento aquilonare,*
*ogni piu bella fantasia gioconda,*
*ogni piu bella immagine scompare,*
*e il dubbio e il freddo e il vuoto mi circonda.'*

*'... I lose hope in the northern wind,*
*every more beautiful joyful phantasy,*
*every more beautiful image disappears,*
*and doubt and cold and flight surround me.'*

– *From* Canto Novo, *Book III, 1, 208 by Gabriele D'Annunzio*

*Translated by Jonathan Steinberg.*

 **EYEWEAR** PUBLISHING

*To my husband Jan and our two daughters, Kasia and Lucy.*

*Special thanks to Rupert Prior for his support in the early stages of this project and to Professor Jonathan Steinberg for his enthusiasm and provision of translations from Italian to English.*

Mara G. Fox was born in London,
spent a childhood in Brighton and now lives in
Cambridge. She has a BA in English and European
Thought and Literature and an MA in Modern British
Literature, was called to the Bar in 1990 and practised as
a criminal barrister for 20 years. Based on her mother's
experiences in Italy during World War II, this is
her first novel.

# Preface

Every once in a while, an absolutely unique book appears, and *The Other Side Of Como* belongs firmly in that category. This novel, based on real events, tells the story of Vivian: a young Englishwoman who falls in love with a handsome Italian in 1930s Camberwell, and, with her husband, sets out to make a new life in Northern Italy. Settling in the centre of a loving Italian family, they run a successful bakery in a beautiful, small village amongst the idyllic lakes and mountains of Lombardy. But then a fascist movement sets up its regime, and the young husband becomes a sympathiser of the anti-fascist resistance. His unbending commitment to that resistance destroys his love, his family and his ties to his wife and children.

Mara G. Fox reconstructs the life of her family by setting it in the context of fascism. Using contemporary photographs, War Office documents and Mussolini's powerful speeches alongside her family sources, she fuses historical texts with the memories and experiences of her own mother and stepfather in the horrors of the Second World War in Italy, in a work that has no parallel in contemporary literature.

The story is historically correct, but no less moving and terrifying for that. Fox illustrates her family's history and that of the country in which they lived, the physical beauty of northern Italy, and the rich array of characters in the community: fascism dividing the society, the family and the young couple.

The Italian war is largely unknown in the English-speaking world and, in my experience, this book is without equal in presenting the intimate experience. Fox has the gift to describe public and private matters, people who act bravely and others who, for complex reasons, get into uniforms and become enemies. I recommend it to English-speaking readers for its richness, humanity and uniqueness as a story.

*Jonathan Steinberg, Emeritus Fellow, Trinity Hall, Cambridge, 18 April 2018*

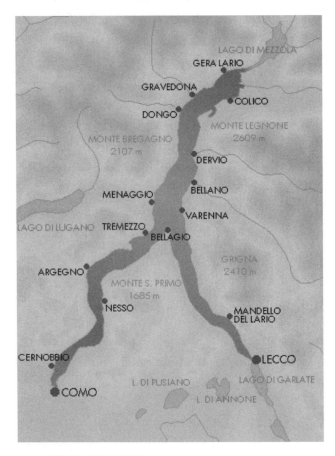

MAP OF COMO AREA

MAP OF ITALY AT WAR

# Prologue

No wheels, no pull-along handle, no zip, no inside pocket. A thoroughly unmodern affair, this black leather suitcase definitely looks old – it's clearly of another time. Rectangular, about the size of a school desk, the edges and corners of the lid are coming apart to reveal the frayed layer of felt between the cracked leather outer and the royal-blue linen interior. The leather-covered metal handle is still tightly fastened to the front by two rusty rings, and the dirty brown International Transport Express label with a big number 38 still clings on beneath it. According to the label, this suitcase has passed through Zurich-Basel-Strasbourg-Hirson-Lille-Calais-Dover to London/Victoria until finally, somehow, down the years, it has come into my hands.

Luckily neither of the locks need keys to undo them and both snap-up catches, although rusted and worn, still open easily. The inside smells musty, filled with the aroma of the past. Papers, photographs, a recipe for something called 'Torta Grigna', an eye-catching red cloth-covered book and letters thrown about inside – bits and pieces of my mother's life in Italy, a life turned upside down by the Second World War. Behind the 'Teach-Yourself-Italian' book there is a photograph of three boys, all in summer shorts and white sunhats, holding buckets and fishing nets. I pick up the seared, frayed Italian flag, holding in my hand this fragment from Mussolini's time, this bitter memento of the German Occupation of Northern Italy.

Why hadn't I opened it before? Why wait so long?

Here among the detritus I see a letter from her eldest son, Leonardo, asking her to send him a particular book for his German lessons, telling her he misses her but he is alright. Saying he loves her. There is no address on the top but at least a location – Mandello. A place to start the hunt for a lost history of an English woman living through difficult times.

A mother hardly known.

# London
## January 1931 to March 1932

Blushing like a hot coal at night, the bright red book sits comfortably in the stout man's hand as he bursts through the door. Vivian Ford starts and sits bolt upright on her chair, her reverie brutally interrupted by the jangling brass bell and cold blast accompanying him.

'It's filthy out there,' he says, forcing the door shut, stamping his feet as he folds his dripping umbrella. He squelches through to the reception desk and presents the book to her. 'I'd like this repaired – look, it's coming apart along the spine,' he says, passing it to her. 'Just here.'

She takes the book gingerly into her right hand as though she expects it to burn her, examining it from different angles. 'Yes, it is in a bad way, isn't it?' she replies, putting it down gently. 'It'll take about a month, as we're a bit behind.'

He looks across his wide fleshy nose at her. 'Oh. That's not like Mason's. Still, never mind. There's no hurry, as I'm not due to go again until September.'

As she slides the costings folder across the desk she glances at the title: *Baedeker's NORTHERN ITALY.*

Waving his fat arm he glances down at her. 'Don't worry. I know roughly how much it'll cost.' Frowning, he fumbles inside his fur-collared coat. 'Here is my card – just add it to my bill.'

She raises her lily-white face, looking at him with expressionless violet eyes, which fluster him enough to ask, 'Are you new here?'

A thin smile splits her lips as she replies, 'I've been here for six months.'

He looks away. 'Must have started just before I came back from my last trip I suppose.' He turns for the door, flipping his left hand in the air. 'Anyway, let me know when it's ready.'

As the door closes she gets up and walks over to the window to stare out at tenacious city grime. White calcified deposits encrust the slimy brick wall opposite and mossy tufts, leeching water, hang about the crevices. The sky casts a slate-grey light down the alleyway opposite and yet the gloom does not hide the bits of rubbish that have been swept up in the vortex of the bitter wind. It's as though the cloud is sitting right on top of her head, bearing down on her, squeezing her heart. Vivian narrows her eyes to focus onto the window itself, onto a particular raindrop slipping down the glass leaving a runnel. She sighs. It's so boring, totally boring, being a receptionist. And she is utterly sick of that miserable wall staring back at her.

Turning abruptly back towards the invitingly compact book, still glowing like a burning ember in the half-light, she picks it up with her right hand and strokes it with her left hand, caressing the cloth cover. Slowly she traces the middle finger along the gold lettering on the front before cautiously opening it up. On the inside page she reads that this Handbook for Travellers by Karl Baedeker also covers Florence, Ravenna and Pisa and that it has 45 maps, 59 plans and diagrams, as well as a panorama. Sitting down, she quickly becomes so absorbed in the introduction about time, money and passports that the mournful light of the room fades away until, to her surprise, it is hometime. After doing her raincoat up to the neck, and tucking a coppery curl of hair inside her beige cloche hat, she bends her head against the biting wind, and leaves.

Setting off down the Old Kent Road she can already hear the throaty voice of her mother. 'Later than usual today, dear'. By the bridge, turning onto the Surrey Canal walk, old brown barge sails whip at the wind as black scuffed hulks crunch against the dockside. A rat slinks slowly across a few logs bunched up against the slippery loading steps as she passes glistening stacks of timber, off-loaded from the Rotherhithe tug. Glancing away from the towpath up the alleyways, where the people who work in the Limekiln industries live, in soot-soiled two-storey buildings, she sees tattered children swarming around in small yards. Tired women toil with bent backs. A little shiver snakes down her spine as she looks away and thinks of the broken fingernails of her mother's hands, reddened by the drudge of domestic work – hurt hands that hardly earn enough to get by. Her weary drawl echoes in her mind again. How many times has she been told, 'Well, I've done my best, girl. It's tough without a husband, so don't you go making the same mistake as me'?

* * *

Vivian lies down on the bed and closes her eyes as loneliness wells up and floods over her. How she misses her best friend – Rosie, with the green eyes and curly dark hair. Letting her mind drift for a moment, she finds that the echo of Mason's brass bell metamorphoses into the school bell. As she dreams, she can almost smell the wet skipping rope and feel the damp knitted bobble hat on her head. In the hell that was the playground she and Rosie stuck together, weathering the Chinese burns inflicted on them, never getting chosen for the team games. They were two of a kind, the odd ones out. All the other girls seemed to have fathers and brothers and sisters but not Rosie, whose father had divorced her mother, and of course she, Vivian herself, had never had one in the first place. Then there was the anxiety about never having enough dinner money. It was always the same at school prayers. When they came to the bit asking to be delivered from evil, she always added, 'and please let fourteen come quickly,' under her breath. How they both longed for the last day of school to arrive.

Vivian had always felt different and Miss Hanley, the headmistress, didn't do difference. Woodwork was for boys; knitting, sewing and weaving for girls. Vivian pricked her fingers on the needles and the thread always ended up in knots, and anyway what on earth was the point in embroidering the word PEGS on a nasty bit of green cloth? She will never forget Miss Hanley. 'Girls don't do woodwork. They sew, that's the way things are. Where is your peg bag? Yes, you do know where it is. You have until tomorrow, otherwise I will see you back in my office.' Next day, on entering the office, she finds Miss Hanley sitting behind her desk, her hair pulled back tightly into a mean little bun. As she stands up her bulky body is revealed. Her head looks like a pea on a drum. 'You know I don't want to do this but you have been told so many times.' She looms over Vivian. 'Hold out your hand'. Her face looks sweaty as she lifts the strap up and thwacks it down on her open palm. Vivian doesn't flinch and as the strap comes down for a second time she is sure she hears Miss Hanley let out a little pant...

A tap on the door chases away the nightmare. 'I've made you a cup of tea, dear.'

'Thank you,' Vivian says, taking the cup from her hand and putting it on the table. Then, suddenly remembering, she gets up and takes out of her bag an envelope containing half her wages. 'Oh, by the way, here you are. I got paid today, '

'Thank you, dear,' her mother says, taking it from the proffered hand.

★ ★ ★

Vivian sits down at the small wooden table in the claustrophobic kitchen, placing her hands along the edges of the red and white checked oil-cloth, watching her mother's plump back working at the stove. An old tan leather belt hangs slack over the brown woollen dress and the few strands of lank yellow hair sticking out of the loose tortoiseshell comb stuck in the back of her head are not flattering; signs of a woman who'd given up. After dishing out the supper at the side of the battered cooker, she passes to Vivian a plate containing two boiled potatoes, a small piece of mutton with a smear of gravy and three carrots, whose riotous orange seems oddly out of place. Flopping down on a chair opposite, her mother asks, 'Work alright today, dear?'

Vivian, looking up into those jaded grey eyes, simply replies. 'Fine, it's better than that shop job,' and pops a carrot into her mouth. Twenty years in this lonely household with the same old plates, same old food – to breathe more easily, Vivian loosens the neck of her blouse – this is her world, all she has ever known – just the two of them, with the odd visit from Uncle Douglas down from Grimsby.

'Is Bill coming round to collect you tomorrow?' her mother asks in that expectant tone Vivian finds so irritating.

'Yes, don't worry. He'll be round.' She leaves the kitchen.

★ ★ ★

Vivian puts the saucer down on the little doily, keeping the cup in her left hand, running the fingers of her other hand through her hair. Her body feels heavy as she sinks down on the padded chair, next to the single loudspeaker perched on top of the radio. For her, this will always be Rosie's room. It was in this room that she last saw Rosie, when she and Jimmy came to say goodbye. She never had understood why Rosie had been in such a hurry to marry Jimmy and go and live in Lancashire. Maybe her mother kept going on about the love of a good man, just as her own mother goes on about what a good catch Bill is.

Rosie said she'd write, and she did, but like all good intentions it gradually faded away. Now the detachment is permanent. Anyway, their lives are so different now. Rosie has a baby and a home to look after.

Vivian looks at the walnut casing and ribbed fretwork of the radio. How many evenings had she and Rosie sat on the floor in here listening to stories on that radio, since their mothers wouldn't let them play out in the street, keeping them close. So much gossiping had gone on in here, so many anxieties aired and characters assassinated in the process. She switches on, no need to turn the dial as the music channel is always the one listened to. Slipping off her black pumps, she leans back and crosses one ankle over another. After a crackle or two the Savoy Hotel dance band comes through, playing 'When You're Smiling' and an involuntary smile crosses her own lips. The band leader's voice sounds rather nasal as he introduces the next tune 'What is This Thing Called Love?' She listens to the melody and thinks about Bill. Judging by the words, nobody seems to know what love is and anyway, it seems to come and go. She and Rosie had spent a long time talking about love and in the end the best they could settle on was, 'it's when you can't imagine life without being with that other person.' She likes Bill and is looking forward to tomorrow evening when they will go down for their usual night at the Dog and Duck. But surely love must be more than just liking someone. Otherwise, what could all the fuss be about?

★ ★ ★

All she has to do when the bell rings is put on her coat and pale brown Tam O'Shanter hat. Bill has both hands on his bicycle handlebars and a grin which goes well with his grey ribbed newsboy's cap. 'Ready for the off, then,' he says, with a cheeky look in his clear blue eyes. She slips her gloves on and they walk side by side.

'Had a good week, then?' he asks.

'Oh, yes. Just the usual. And you?'

'Yes. You know Ticky Snacks Ltd?'

'Yes, the pie man whose pies are advertised as '"Made as Muvver Makes 'Em"?'

'That's the one. Well a big company called J. Lyons has taken them over and I've been asked to do the accounts.'

'What does that mean for you?'

'More money,' he says, putting the bike against the pub wall. He opens the door for her and they move through the warm fug of the Public Bar to a table in the corner.

Vivian hands him her coat and sits down, noticing that as he reaches up to the coat hooks his black braces peek out from under his light tweed waistcoat. He throws his cap on the table in front of her and, with a wide smile that lights up his open face, asks 'What shall we have tonight, then?'

'The usual. A half of mild and some crisps.' Vivian watches him go over to the bar. The mirror behind the bar is alive with the reflection of rows of glasses, bottles, stacked matches and packets of Woodbine cigarettes. The barman picks up a tankard and puts his right hand on one of the brass-topped white china handles, pumping it until the glass is full. Vivian eyes the two distinctive red, white and blue Smith's crisps packets, looking forward to unfurling the little blue twist packet with the salt inside. 'Cheers,' she says, chinking her glass against his. 'Is Jack coming tonight?'

'Later, so shall we get started before anyone else does?' Bill nods towards the dartboard. 'You go first.'

Vivian takes her place behind the line, a few feet from the board, ignoring the scowls of one or two men who always make it plain that they disapprove of a female presence in the Public Bar, let alone one that pretends she can play darts. Rather enjoying being the subject of such interest and disdain, she rolls the torpedo-shaped dart in her fingers, feeling the coldness of the heavy brass barrel and relishing the red, white and blue of the tail feathers. Lifting her right arm, so that she can throw the dart at eye-level, she lines it up with the outer double ring. Tipping forward, and with a steady hand, she launches the dart, which lands midway between the double and triple ring. She picks up the second dart and tries again, just missing once more. Irritated by the feeling that her own failure would be giving pleasure to the scowlers, she takes a swig of beer. Finally, taking her time, she throws the third dart and it hits the double ring. While Bill chalks up the score on the chalkboard she calmly removes the three darts and, with a triumphant gleam in her eye, hands them to him.

Vivian, sitting on the saddle of the bicycle as Bill walks alongside, glances at him.

'I wonder what happened to Jack tonight?'

'I don't know. Maybe had to work late.'

Vivian slides off the seat as Bill leans over the handlebars of his bicycle towards her. She lets him give her a quick kiss on the lips before turning her face to the side.

'You know, I think you are the most beautiful girl in the world. Are you sure you can't come to the cinema this weekend?

'Maybe,' she says, squeezing his arm. As she turns the key in the door, she looks back and shouts back. 'Why don't you find out what's on, then?'

★ ★ ★

Vivian takes the Baedeker out of her bag and puts it on the side, away from the food.

Knowing nobody would miss it over the weekend, she has done what she shouldn't have, and borrowed it.

Under the ticking clock, dinner forks scratch against china. Her mother fills the pregnant silence. 'What's that red book?'

'Oh, just something from Mason's that looks rather interesting.'

'What's it about?'

'Italy.'

'I might have guessed.' Her mother finishes chewing a bit of lamb rump before continuing. 'Got anything lined up for the weekend?'

'I'm going down to Camberwell Green tomorrow – can I bring something back?' Vivian replies in a light tone.

'Not that Polti's Café again?' her mother snorts.

'Yes, I like it.'

Her mother looks up. 'So I noticed.'

'There's a white tablecloth on every table, doesn't matter if it's small or not, and potted palms in each corner and candles and carnations. You get real coffee there.' Vivian's eyes light up as she describes it, both hands fluttering in the air.

A chair leg screeches against the cold stone as her mother, irritated by such animated gestures and breathless enthusiasm, stands up quickly to clear the plates. 'Fancy foreign nonsense,' she mutters as she slops the dishes around in the murky water, and looks back at Vivian. 'Bring back some butter and cheese from Brown's, would you, dear?'

★ ★ ★

Camel coat buttoned up, velvet collar brushed and hands carefully encased in smooth black leather gloves, Vivian turns left onto Camberwell Green Road. Things are always lively down here – all those rich people in Denmark Hill and Herne Hill need dairies, butchers, grocers, cafés and restaurants to service their tables and delight their palates. Bare branched trees stand sculpted against the winter sky and lively white clouds scud by as Vivian examines the pasticciere section of the Polti café-restaurant window – an enticing array of chocolate cakes, amaretti biscuits and festive, shocking-red Panettone tins. Flitting to the entrance, she turns the dark brass handle of the door, a swirling rose with a raised inner centre and matching escutcheon – a stylish entrance to a marquetry-panelled world so different from that of the English 'caff'. Silvered cutlery glints from the side table and sharply-folded napkins wait to be laid out at lunch-time. Palm fronds brush her legs as she catches sight of her own tall figure, as she settles down into a corner seat under the large mirror ornately framed with wooden carvings of fir cones, fruits and flowers.

The waiter, bow-tied and plump, comes over and with a small bow says, 'A black coffee as usual, Madam?'

'Yes please, and an amaretti biscuit as well' she replies with a sophisticated little smile. Lifting the Baedeker out of her bag, she opens it carefully and settles down to learn how to plan a tour; that, in the height of summer, excessive exposure to sun should be avoided, and coloured spectacles may be an advantage. That it is also important not to over-exert oneself, so as to avoid malaria. She hovers the tongs over the little silver bowl, snips up a sugar lump and plops it into the aromatic coffee. Turning the page, she reads to find that begging is always one of those national nuisances to which the traveller in Italy must accustom himself and that beggars of the importunate sort should be dismissed with 'niente' or by a gesture of negation. Slightly offended by the tone of superiority, she moves on through the guide, which has many little fold-out maps but no pictures. She picks a city at random – Ravenna, learning that it is a town that Lord Byron preferred to all others in Italy, and where a famous Italian poet, Dante Alighieri, was buried: his tomb is the thing to see. The interrupting clatter of table-laying finally reaches her ears and, realising it is time to leave, she steps out into the frigid air determining to buy a copy of this book for herself; to have her own little bit of Italy.

★ ★ ★

Vivian feels heady in the bright spring morning, the sweet smell of greening grass causing her step to quicken as she makes her Saturday morning pilgrimage to Polti's. She sits differently today, looking inwards, towards the service area, and that is when she first sees him, bent over the cake display cabinet. Pointy-featured with a pencil moustache, slicked-back, straight, black hair and pursed full lips, he is intensely focused on placing a tall, spongy cake in just the right place. Clearly feeling her inquisitive look, he lifts his head and smiles at her. She averts her face and then, slowly, as if compelled by a magnetic force, she turns back again to gaze back at those eyes, glittering in the uplight of the cake display cabinet. 'Giulio, pronto,' shouts a voice from the kitchen area, and, winking at her, he is gone, and it seems to her as though the sun has gone behind a cloud. With a sharp shift of the shoulder she turns her head to face the usual plump waiter.

He smiles. 'Coffee as usual, I presume. And what about our specialty, today, Madam?'

She recovers herself. 'Why not – what is it?'

'Torta Grigna, made by our new pasticciere, Giulio Ricci,' and as he walks away says over his shoulder. 'All the way from Lake Como.'

With an air of excitement she picks up her very own precious Baedeker – at last, a real reason to look something up: she reads that Como is the most beautiful of the lakes, the western leg being full of gay villas belonging to the Milanese aristocracy, surrounded by luxuriant gardens and vineyards, fragrant oleanders and laurel growing wild. Shutting the book and laying her left hand against her long neck she pulls the plate towards her. Light and almondy, the Torta Grigna is soft on her tongue, and as she closes her eyes she remembers a photograph she has seen in a different book. It was called the Villa Melzi, a perfectly proportioned white building with an ornate orangery at its side, and peacocks stepping about lawns that flow down to the lakeshore. She glances periodically at the kitchen door, but the new pasticciere is not to be seen again that morning. But those eyes, that look, his hair, his lips – she can't get them out of her mind. All through the week, her heart hangs on the possibility in that wink.

The following Saturday, her stomach fluttering with expectation, she makes her way to Polti's and there it is, standing brash and bold in the window, given pride of place on its own silver plate, a large notice alongside: *Gold Medal Winner: THE TORTA GRIGNA*. She goes in and it seems to her he must have been waiting, as he is there straight away, coming towards her with one hand in his pocket. He is slender, a few inches taller than her and she can instantly tell he is self-assured, not given to error, turns boredom into amusement and regards silence as a space to be filled. On pulling the chair out for her, he brushes the seat with a napkin. 'Same as last week I hope, Madam?'

'Oh, yes, please.'

Supplanting the waiter, who doesn't seem to mind, he carries over a slice of his magic torta, with a small fork and a cup of coffee. He bows his head a little. 'Vivian, isn't it?'

She looks up and flushes. 'Yes, Giulio, it is – how did you know?'

He glances down at the red book she has put open on the table. 'It's there, written on your book.'

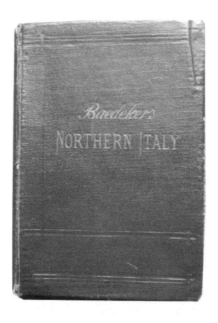

Crimson nails flashing dangerously, she slowly cuts a piece of torta with the small fork, and raises it before her parted lips. 'It is delicious, what's in it?'

Straightening his back and lifting his right hand, as if engaging in a poetic recital, he begins. 'It has all the ingredients of the mountain: almonds and round hazelnuts from the Langhe in Piedmont, flour and eggs from the land, yeast. From these we make the Torta, with small crevasses like the Grigna mountains, a soft covering of icing sugar on the top like a light snowfall.' Lowering his hand, eyes gleaming with pride, he looks down at her. 'In 1912, my father Luigi won a Gold Medal for this recipe at the World Exposition in Florence.'

With an ironic little smile, she looks up. 'Well, how on earth can I resist, then?'

The next Saturday he has a map with him and on opening it sits down opposite her. 'I'll show you where the Grigna mountains are.' Slim, hairy hands dart over the mountain ranges. 'Here is Grigna Settentrionale, the biggest one, and here is Grigna Meridionale, another big one. See this, Piani Resinelli, there is built a little mountain house.' He raises his forefinger and then stabs it down. 'Here – it's in my family'.

'Is that where they live?' she asks.

He leans a little closer. 'No, here on the eastern leg of the lake in Mandello-del-Lario, just above Lecco.' He looks up, a lively smile revealing a row of crooked but perfectly white teeth. 'Resinelli is just for fun.'

She smiles into warm brown eyes. 'What are you doing such a long way from home then?'

Like a tarantella dancer with his scarf he stands up suddenly, whisking the map away. 'Seeing the world, escaping Mr. Mussolini.' With a serious look and a small cough to the back of his hand he asks. 'Now, Madam, what can I get you today?'

★ ★ ★

Books come and go at Masons, the rich man's Baedeker is repaired and returned to him, forms are filled in and days drag by; still, nearly Saturday, the day of the car ride. Feeling skittish, knowing she will see him soon, her heart beats faster than usual. Parked at a slight angle to the kerb, the running-board of the little black Austin 7 shines in the aftermath of a late April shower. Watching Giulio folding back the beige canvas top she laughs as he pulls on a brown leather aviator's hat and slides racing goggles over his head. She jumps in beside him, he revs up the engine and toots the horn while she tilts a winter-white face towards the sun, and they whirl off, up hills and down streets, past pink-blossomed trees and finely gardened villas until, pulling the car up with a skidding flourish, they reach Ruskin Park.

Slipping a bright orange cigarette packet marked 'Macedonian' out of his trouser pocket, Giulio offers her one.

'Later, perhaps.' She watches him remove a pocket petrol lighter from his jacket, bending his head to the right, twisting his mouth sideways as he rasps a tiny wheel all the time with his thumb until a burst of flame lights the end of his cigarette.

Inhaling deeply, he looks up directly at her and releases a stream of smoke out of the corner of his mouth. 'How long have you lived here?'

She looks away. 'I was born in Stepney, within the sound

of the Bow Bells, which makes me something called a Cock-
ney. And you – how long are you here for?' she asks.

'I could only get papers for a year, that's all. The Fascists
won't let you go for any longer, unless they want to get rid of
you'.

'What about your family – don't they miss you?'

He kicks a stone onto the grass. 'They're quite proud. I'm
the first in the family to go abroad.' He gives her a sidelong
glance. 'I do miss my motorbike though'.

She turns back towards him in shock. 'What? You miss a
machine more than your parents?'

He takes her elbow and points her towards Toni's ice-
cream cart over to the right. As they walk towards it, he asks,
'Doesn't your father have a motorbike?'

'No, he died before I was born,' she lies.

'That's a sad thing.' After the silence he continues. 'In my
town there's a factory, Moto Guzzi, so everyone's got a motorbike.' Flicking the cigarette stub high in the air, he says.
'Summer sun and motorbikes – made for each other'. Toni's
white coat dazzles in the sunlight as he whips a couple of cones
out of a tin on top of the cart and spoons in the strawberry
ice-cream. Giulio sticks his tongue out and licks the ice-cream
in a circle. 'Ah, reminds me of home, ice-creams by the lake.'

'Is that where you learned to be a pasticciere?'

'Yes, I was always in Papa's café. I used to go with him to
the biscuit factory he owned, back then. One day the café will
be mine.'

Back at the car, he turns to face her. 'Would you like to
come round tomorrow, and we can make a Torta Grigna together?'

'Oh, I would love to, but are you sure you want to let me in on the magic recipe?' She smiles coquettishly.

He arches his eyebrow. 'I think my secret would be safe with you.' He jots down his address on the back of the now-empty cigarette packet and hands it to her, before opening the car door. 'Is around three o'clock alright?'

After sliding the address into her imitation crocodile skin handbag, she snaps the brass clasps together and, barely able to hide the little thrill in her voice, replies. 'Yes, perfect.'

★ ★ ★

Vivian spends longer than usual getting ready but, aware she is going to be baking, doesn't want to overdress. She slips on a casual blue sweater with a black necklace nestling over the collarbone and, rather daringly, a pair of grey slacks. She ties her hair back in a pony tail, powders her face and even puts a little dab of the precious Chanel No. 5 she has had to save up so long for on her neck; after all, this is a special event. Knowing her mother would notice that she was rather dressed up for just a Sunday walk, she is prepared.

'You look smarter than usual dear, where are you off to?'

'I've made an arrangement with a girl I met at Polti's. We are going to bake a special cake together.'

'What, in the café?'

'No, in her house.'

'What's her name?'

'Julia.'

'You know, Vivian, it isn't a good idea to make a spectacle of yourself by wearing trousers. People talk.'

'I don't mind if they do,' Vivian replies as she goes out of the door.

★ ★ ★

Vivian discovers that the Victorian villa is only just around the corner from Polti's. She pushes the latch on the wrought-iron gate and walks up red-and-cream chequered tiles to a blue door. After giving two little taps on the doorknocker (shaped like a lion rampant), she steps back. Giulio opens it and simply stands still, unable to take his eyes off her.

'Can I come in, then?'

'Sorry. Come up.' Leading her through the shiny hallway upstairs, he points, 'I'm in here.'

Once inside, the first thing she notices are his work clothes flung across the back of a wicker-seat chair. The window is open and the fresh spring air has almost blown away the smoke of the cigarette end still smouldering in the ashtray. The dresser takes up a lot of space and the coal stove juts out into the room, making it more than a little cramped.

'How long did it take you to get here?' he asks, watching her legs cross, one over the other, as she settles on the scuffed leather settee.

'Oh, not long, twenty minutes or so. What's the situation in this house?' she asks.

'The landlady is an elderly widow and I'm just another lodger.' he says, sitting on the arm of the settee. 'But, more importantly, tell me: do you bake at home?'

'No. My mother sometimes makes Yorkshire Parkin, but I don't like that. It's got black treacle and oats in it.'

'Good,' he says, jumping up and beckoning her towards the kitchen. 'So I've got a complete beginner – my favourite.'

Following in his footsteps, her eyes scan his back, admiring the way he moves his body with a soft flexibilty. She looks at the various ingredients all carefully laid out on the dresser, notices the table, kept spick and span, and the little saucepan on top of the cooker, the oven having already been lit. 'Are you always so neat and tidy?'

'Yes, you take care when you are baking, unless you want to risk a disaster,' he replies, lifting two white baker's aprons from the back of a chair. He ties one around his own waist and then moves behind her. Her skin tingles as she feels his warm breath on the back of her neck. He then reaches round her waist, taking his time before pulling the apron strings and tying a bow. She turns as he asks. 'Your perfume – what is it?'

'Chanel No. 5. Do you like it?'

'It's lovely,' he says, leading her towards a mixing bowl. 'Now, would you mix this cornflour starch and white flour together with your fingers?'

She plunges her hands in enthusiastically so that a cloud of white dust flies up in the air powdering her arms and blue sweater. 'Oh no, look what I've done. I'm so clumsy.'

'It's a beginner's mistake,' he says, his hands lingering to brush the flour off her sweater.

They move over to the cooker and together watch the lump of butter he has put into the small saucepan slowly soften and liquefy. Vivian admires the agility of his hands and the sureness of touch as he beats the already-weighed-out sugar into the warm butter and tips in the ground almonds and hazelnuts, as well as the flour mixture.

'Let's separate the eggs,' he says. 'You can then stir in the yolks whilst I whip the egg whites and fold them in.' He interweaves his hands in illustration. Letting Vivian add the salt and yeast, he flours and butters a baking tin. With the mixture safely in the oven they untie their aprons and sit down. Riding the tide of admiration obvious in her eyes, he smiles. 'So that is how to make the magic Torta Grigna.'

When it is time to leave, Giulio, in an open gesture, holds out both his hands towards her. 'So what shall we do next? Do you like dancing?'

She twirls around in a circle. 'Yes, I do! Where?'

He catches her hand. 'Lovejoy's, the cabaret club on the side of the Rosemary Branch. The fat waiter took me there once – it's good.'

He puts the Torta Grigna, wrapped up in a special grease-proof paper, in her left hand.

'Here, this is for your mother, with my compliments.'

★ ★ ★

A few days later, having come in from work and lain on the bed for a while, Giulio gets up. He fills the round cracked basin with icy cold water and shaves for the second time that day. After combing his brilliantined hair over to the right, he pats on his favourite after-shave, squares his shoulders and begins admiring his profile in the mirror. Brushing at the crinkles in his suit and sliding a small red rose into the buttonhole, he smirks at his own romantic gesture as he trips lightly down the stairs in his shiny shoes.

Watching her walking towards him along the Green, he

admires her loping, easy gait: he sees a dancing woman. A good height, too – his mother would only reach up to her shoulders. Her glossy auburn hair is pulled back off her face and held in place by a thin piece of blue silky material over which natural curls flow; how she would love the silk from Como, he thinks, smiling into her long-lashed velvet eyes, thinking of kissing those perfectly formed lips.

He takes her right arm as they saunter off to Southampton Way and enter the long, low-ceilinged room at the side of The Rosemary Branch. It takes some time for his eyes to become accustomed to the dingy light cast by the flaming gas in wall brackets. The stage is bathed in an eerie blue glow as they make their way towards an empty table and chairs near the front. The Chairman of Events, in a shiny three-piece suit, tie at an angle, sits facing the audience with his legs open so that his paunch can hang comfortably in between. There is an upright piano at the side of the stage and a small, thin, bald man is playing a jazzy tune while people hold conversations above the din. A sweaty shirt-sleeved waiter dashes around in the blue smoke haze holding above his head a tray full of beer and sandwiches. 'Scusi, cameriere,' Giulio shouts at him, just as the pianist stops playing. A few heads turn. 'You alright with beer?' he asks Vivian, who nods her head. The Chairman of Events raps his hammer on a little table and introduces a man who sings a song about a ukelele. While they wait for the sandwiches and beer, Giulio continues to watch Vivian discreetly as she takes out a little gold compact from her handbag and pouts her lips voluptuously towards a small mirror before carefully refreshing the bright red lipstick and then sucking her mouth inwards like a cat's bottom. He smiles at her knowingly. When at last a dancing tune comes on, Giulio stands up. 'Come on, let's go.'

She leaps up into his arms and he holds her close, leaning her hips in towards him – how fluid her movements are, her innate sense of rhythm easily matching his own flamboyant moves. The remains of the beer grows warm as, flirting and laughing, enchanting each other with every twist and turn, time flies away, until it is time to go, and he is driving her home, pulling up a few yards from her house. She sits still, prolonging the moment of departure, until he leans over the steering wheel and, turning her head gently towards him, slowly kisses those luscious red lips, brushing his hand lightly over her right breast.

★ ★ ★

'You're late, where've you been?' says her mother, pink candlewick dressing gown flung over a crumpled nightie. She comes closer, slippers shuffling on wooden planks, sniffing at her. 'You stink of beer and cigarettes.'

'Mind your own business,' Vivian spits out, flouncing into her bedroom.

But her mother follows, pulling roughly at her arm, the pupils in her eyes small and tight. 'Don't think I don't know you're seeing some Italian waiter.'

Vivian snatches her arm away. 'Oh no, I'm not – he's a master pasticciere.'

'A what?'

'A master baker – his father won prizes back in Italy.'

'If you believe that you'd believe anything,' her mother says with a mocking smile.

Vivian shouts out. 'Leave me alone,' throwing herself onto the bed as her mother walks out of the room, shaking her head.

★ ★ ★

'I don't bluff and don't sell smoke. The revolution is not a jack-in-the-box which pops up at will... History, made up of remote facts, teaches people little but daily events could be more useful. Now the daily events teach us that you make revolutions with, not against, the army; with arms not without arms; with movements of disciplined squads, not amorphous masses called to demonstrate in the public square.'

*– Benito Mussolini, Bologna Fascist Speech, April 1921*

Having slashed the envelope open with his penknife, Giulio throws it onto the small wooden table, removes the letter, pulls out a chair and sits down next to the sink full of un-washed dishes, to begin reading.

15th May 1931
Mandello

Darling Giulio,

Papa and I are missing you and the boat needs some patching up but how is London for you? There has been some trouble at the café as Carlo was sweeping up outside when Giovanni Farace passed by with his blackshirt friends. He kicked the brush out of his hands and they all chanted communisti bastardo. Carlo called him a big mouth and punched Giovanni in the face and broke his nose – blood everywhere and it won't end there. It's not like Carlo and his mama is more worried about what will happen next than having to take the Fascist oath to stay teaching at the school.

Things have got a bit better with the sugar and flour supplies so maybe Il Duce will turn things around for us after all but Papa does worry a lot now that the biscuit factory has gone. The other thing you will want to hear is there is a new Moto Guzzi sporty model – GT 17 – so everyone wants one. I still think your old Normale looks more beautiful and it stands quite lonely waiting for you.

Are you coming home soon?

Your loving Mama

Throwing the letter aside, guilt seizes his heart; like a rat deserting a sinking ship he has run away to England to have fun, leaving his family and his childhood friends at the mercy of the cult of Mussolini, at the beck and call of the Fascist party and its lickspittles. Feeling agitated, he grabs his work trousers from the back of the chair, pulling them on quickly, and after throwing a shirt hastily on his back, stamps down the stairs, vowing to go home – sometime soon.

★ ★ ★

'A scrawny bird, this one. Not much flesh on it,' says Vivian's mother, as she pushes the stuffing inside the chicken. Wiping grease from her hands, she throws a grubby cloth on the side. 'I saw Susan today.'

Vivian mutters. 'Oh, yes'.

'She's getting married'.

'Oh, that's nice.'

'Here, you can peel these potatoes if you want.' Her mother pushes a chipped enamel bowl towards Vivian. 'To Fred, you know, the butcher's boy.'

'How many do you want?'

'Four.' After putting the bleeding giblets into a saucepan her mother moves to the sink to wash her hands, and slyly says. 'Isn't it time you thought about such things?'

Vivian begins peeling. 'Probably is.'

Her mother puts the chicken in the roasting tin and turns round. 'Best to stay local, stick with the familiar. You know Bill is a decent young man, and accountancy's a good trade.'

dilly and it's got a famous Artist's Room upstairs. You'll be pleased to hear she's got as much style as any of the Milanese girls – I've got the local tailor, Romano, to make me a new suit – he's going to give me a special price.

Tell Papa it won't be long before I am home again to sail on the lake and walk in the mountains. Please make sure the motorbike is started up now and again or I may have trouble with it. I'm hoping my car will be strong enough for such a long journey.

Your loving Giulio.

★ ★ ★

After pulling the left rim of her blue and white striped cloche hat down over her left eye and adjusting the feather so that it sticks straight up on the right hand side, she strides out of the house. A little smile plays on her lips – all those trips over to Petticoat Lane market, all that rummaging around in the second-hand clothes stalls and evenings spent hunched over her dreaded sewing, have finally paid off. She can feel her mother's eyes on her back but still leaves without a look over the shoulder. There he is, waiting for her and looking *so* stylish in a charcoal-grey, double-breasted suit, a slim tie striped green and brown, and a pale pink carnation in his lapel. With a large open smile on her lips she leans forward. 'Where are you taking me then?'

With a sneaky glance, he opens the car door for her. 'To the most magnificent restaurant in the world.'

'It's fantastic,' she gasps, looking up at the signature over the entrance: 'PAGANI'S'. 'And every bit of it's decorated!' Walking through the four illuminated archways, she runs her hand along the two-toned glazed tiles, tracing the shamrock design with her fingers, 'I love it all!'

'It's Art Nouveau style,' Giulio informs her.

Sniffing at the sweet, woody aroma of cigar, Vivian enters the blue-wallpapered room on the first floor. Making his way through the buzzing clientele, an impeccably dressed waiter guides them to a table by the window and graciously pulls out a chair for her.

Feeling like Cinderella at the ball, she finds herself stroking the soft blue curtains discreetly with her fingers, and gazing with dazzled eyes around the room, entranced by the liveliness of the animated diners. 'This is wonderful. Have you been here before?' she asks.

Opening the leather-covered menu, Giulio glances up, resting his left hand on the pristine white tablecloth. 'No, but I've heard of it. It's popular with artists and musicians'. Pointing his finger and pursing his lips he bends over. 'Now let me see, what shall we have?' At last, Vivian chooses the famous borscht soup and a partridge casserole followed by lemon sorbet, whilst Giulio orders hors-d'oeuvre a la maison, a steak Pagani and Curaçao soufflé together with a red wine from Tuscany – a Montepulciano.

Giulio takes an embossed silver cigarette case out of his jacket pocket, opens it and offers her one.

'Oh, that's very sophisticated,' Vivian says, looking at the case and taking a cigarette. Aware that his eyes are on her lips, she leans forward for a light, inhales slightly and looks up at him, managing not to cough.

'It's a present from my Uncle, Alberto, he likes nice things.'

At the table on the right is a blonde, holding a tortoiseshell cigarette-holder at a dramatic angle as she languidly converses. Vivian imagines she is a husky-voiced singer usually found in a long black dress and white elbow length gloves, her golden hair shimmering in the spotlight. Opposite the blonde, there is a middle-aged man with a clipped beard and bald head, whose dancing hands are full of little gestures, his eyes darting about, his lips sucking on a cigar. 'Tell me then, Giulio, that man at the table to my left, what do you think he does to earn a living?'

After a slow turn of the head and a furtive glance Giulio looks back at her. 'Well, from his movements, I think he's modelling himself on a famous Italian poet, Gabriele D'Annunzio, who said all beautiful people were bald'.

Vivian widens her eyes. 'But, bald is ugly.'

'Well, not in his case. He was a grand seducer, a warrior, a superstitious chancer who tossed coins to make big decisions.' Leaning towards her conspiratorially Giulio whispers, 'He wore perfume and kept cocaine in a little box in his waistcoat pocket – a true Italian hero.'

'Yes, but what about the young woman he is with?'

Giulio smirks knowingly. 'Oh, he'll have her for breakfast.'

The succulent partridge is a perfect foil to the sweet, blood-coloured borscht. Sighing, Vivian puts the fork down on the empty plate. 'How come you Italians are so good at restaurants?'

Dabbing the napkin to his mouth, Giulio replies. 'There's a history of Italians running away from the too-cold valleys in winter, up through Paris to London. They bring with them their chestnut specialities, their skills as chocolatiers and so on.' He points his left forefinger towards his chest. 'Just like me, that's what I'm doing with my Torta Grigna.'

The lemon sorbet fizzes lightly on her palate. 'Are you going to stay here, then?'

He pulls his head up. 'I don't know. I've thought about it'. Then raising his chin, he looks past her, dreamily. 'But there would be no mountains, no blue sky,' then, aware of her enraptured eyes, he begins moving his hands in little wavelike motions, D'Annunzio style. 'No brightly coloured small boats on the water, no skiing, no hunting, no family, no orange sunsets on Monte Grigna.' Visiting upon her the sudden charm of his smile, he cups her left hand in his, looking into her eyes, and leans forward. 'But I wouldn't want to miss sitting opposite such a beautiful woman on her birthday.' He raises his glass. 'Here's to you,' and her heart flutters as it succumbs to the overwhelming fascination of this foreigner.

Vivian, draining the last dregs of the Coffee Pagani, lets her tongue linger on the final drop of the almond liqueur, as the manager, dapper in his dark suit, comes to their table. He stoops a little towards her.

'Is the Signorina ready for her birthday surprise?'

Vivian affects an appropriately startled expression before being led to The Artists Room. It is only 8ft wide, has a small table and red velvet drapes at the window – a perfect size for a private dining room. On the walls, at head height and protected by glass panels, are writings, drawings, jokes and music – pieces of fame frozen in aspic. The Manager proudly points out the names of Oscar Wilde, Sarah Bernhardt, Caruso and Nellie Melba as Giulio grabs her elbow.

'Look here Vivian, this is Denza and see written above are the words of his famous songs – all Italians love singing these.'

She smiles as a feeling of sophisticated privilege sweeps over her until sadly Giulio is saying, 'Bellissimo, mille grazie' as he guides her downstairs into the warm evening air. Huddling together and laughing, their footfalls echoing along the pavement, his soft breath close to her ear, she hears him say.

'Let's go back to mine.'

Silent anticipation fills the car; she leans her neck, pale as a swan, against the back of the car seat and fiddles with her pearl earring. Unspoken hopes hang in the air as they mount the stairs, as the key enters the lock. Giulio slips her jacket off her shoulders and hangs it on a hook before turning and coming towards her. Smelling of tobacco and chocolate, he puts his forefinger under her chin, moving her head upwards towards him, murmuring.

'Stay, stay with me tonight'.

Leaning forward, she kisses his lips, feels his tongue inside her mouth, his hands sliding under her blouse. Feeling a growing sense of urgency, she wants more. As his lean body begins moving rhythmically against her she wants her breath taken away. But when he begins pressing her hard against the wall, pushing her legs apart and lifting her skirt, like a shot in the dark, an image rears up in the front of her mind, a hallucinogenic glimpse of her mother's careworn face and those red hands, her warning echoing in her mind. 'Don't, don't make the same mistake as me.' Stiffening, she pushes him away.

'Get off – get off!' An alarm bell of self-preservation casting aside her desire. Looking at his stunned face, she moves forwards and leans her head against his panting chest, muttering, 'I'm so sorry... I shouldn't have come back here tonight... I'm really sorry.' Raising tearful eyes to his, she says, 'Please give me a lift home.'

Awkward silence fills the air as he pulls the car up at the kerb. 'I'm really sorry, too'.

Putting her hand over his lips, she gently kisses the side of his face before slipping out of the car and walking away.

★ ★ ★

The next day, shoulders hunched, she walks slowly past the row of shops, turning up the lane to the side entrance of St Giles Church in Camberwell Church Street. Vivian pushes the rickety wooden gate shut behind her. On closing the squeaky main door and noticing she is alone, she sits in her favourite pew, right in the middle, since this is a good position to see the Ruskin stained-glass window. Not being religious by nature, the biblical content is of no interest to her but the deep, rich reds and violets in the glass are what she has come for, usually so comforting, so soothing. But not today, as, here in the quiet solitude, she begins crying, her liquid eyes losing focus in the overall mosaic effect of the glass. Amongst the stale remnants of flowers, she feels bereft. She has lost him. How could he forgive her for leading him on. A wave of shame spreads over her as she recalls the fun they had last night, his intense kisses and her stupid response. Why should he bother with her? There are plenty of other fish in the sea, for him. But he is the only one *she* loves; he is so different, so fresh and daring, so beautiful and she has thrown it all away, letting her mother's sour words intervene. And yet, look at the poor woman's life. A baby could so easily happen to her, Vivian, too.

She blows her nose. What should I do now? Go back to Polti's, maybe. After all, if he loves me he will forgive me, won't he? If not, well, I've had a lucky escape, surely. If only Rosie was here to talk to. She begins to focus on the altar – perhaps I should say a little prayer. After all, you never know, there could be someone up there. She goes down on her knees, folds her fingers together, closes her eyes and mumbles. 'Dear God, if you're listening, let him forgive me – give me another chance, please, please.' She stays a while like that, wondering what on earth to say next, for, isn't God supposed to see into your soul ? She stands up suddenly, feeling silly. And yet, it is with a transitory flicker of hope in her heart that she slips silently out of the church door.

* * *

After hanging his suit in the cupboard, Giulio jumps into the bed, lying rigid in the dark. He can still remember the scent of Vivian's perfume. Imagines gazing into her mesmeric eyes, feeling clammy as his body heat rises, tasting her mouth, touching her hard nipples with his fingertips, clutching the pillow and staining the sheets. Getting up early next morning, flinging on some old clothes, he sets out to take a walk along the Thames. Amidst the aroma of mud and summer river-rot he pulls his black Como Borsalino hat low down on his brow to block out the sharp metallic gleam of the water, passes a skulking dog, and lights a cigarette. Images of her flood through his brain, her soft voice permeates his head as he wonders what to do next. Can I just forget her? If not, would she marry me if I ask her? If she said yes, would she follow me home? Maybe I should stay here, open a café of my own? Flicking his cigarette end to join the cluster of others jammed up against the gutter, he lights up again and walks on. He stops abruptly, examining his muddy boots, before moving on again. She loves me, I know she does. I want her; I can't bear to leave her. Leaning, one leg up on a railing, lighting yet another cigarette, he inhales deeply, slowly, letting his mind go blank, leaving room for his heart alone to speak. I love her. He walks on and punching the air shouts out, 'I'll ask her to marry me!' A sense of relief floods through him. Yet his hands still feel sticky as he fiddles with the coins in his pocket, and the tincture of the light is giving him a headache.

★ ★ ★

There's still another dilemma lurking; he walks one way and then the other – to go or to stay, Italy or exile. A new life in London away from Fascism seems attractive, but how could he leave his family, his own country, his mountains? Backwards and forwards he goes. He thinks he remembers D'Annunzio once saying that some things are so difficult to decide, you may as well toss a coin. Perhaps he had a point. He draws a penny out of his pocket, looks at the bearded head of King George V before turning it over and examining Britannia ruling the waves – heads for home then, tails for England. Sitting it on his crooked thumb he spins it high, watching each glinting twist until it flips down, clips the edge of the tow path, and spins off into the sweating, oily water, but not before he sees which side is up. His heart lightens as he turns for home, knowing he has got the answer he really wants.

★ ★ ★

On arriving home from work, Vivian finds her mother waiting for her, standing awkwardly in the hallway clutching an envelope, placing it in her hand, whispering conspiratorially, 'He's been round, left this for you.' Snatching it ungraciously, Vivian runs into her bedroom and slams the door, tearing it open with shaking hands and churning stomach.

27<sup>th</sup> July 1931
London

My darling Vivian,

I am truly sorry your birthday ended badly Saturday night and that I was to blame for that. I should
never have done such a thing, please forgive me.

As much as I have enjoyed my time in London my family need my help and it is time for me
to think about home. But the question I ask is can
I bear to leave you and I realise I don't want to live
my life without you because I love you. You are
the one for me. Will you come to Italy and marry
me?

I know it would be a big decision for you to
leave your mother and England and I don't want
you to think life in Italy would be easy as it is a
poor country with too many mouths to feed. Benito Mussolini controls everything and it is difficult
to go against him and his kind. Still, life on the
lake is beautiful, with boating in the summer and
skiing in the winter and Mama and Papa would
welcome you.

I will be waiting for you at the Café.

Your loving Giulio,
*PS I could bake Torta Grigna all the time for you.*

Kissing the signature over and over again, holding it to her heart, tears running down her cheeks, Vivian runs out to find her mother, the excited words tumbling out. 'He's asked me, he's asked me, he wants to marry me!'

Her mother's voice remains steady at first. 'Oh, that's lovely, dear, where will you live?'

'He's asked me to go to Italy.' Seeing her mother unable to hide the shock on her face, she says, 'What's the matter? You should be happy for me. You know, Italy – beautiful Italy?'

'Yes... but it's what I feared... it's so far away... can't he stay here?'

'No, he can't, and I've got to go.' Vivian blurts out, putting her hand on her mother's arm. 'You see, I love him.'

Her mother turns her head away to hide the tears, mumbling. 'It's just that I've heard bad things about Italy, that's all.'

★ ★ ★

Giulio, at Polti's, having decided to bake a Torta di Riso, sets about peeling and grinding the sweet and bitter almonds together with some sugar. Having already cooked rice in milk, he adds almonds and lemon peel and sets it aside to cool. Going out of the kitchen into the café area, he sits down on a stool, glancing up every time the door opens. Why isn't she here yet? Going back into the kitchen, he stirs three eggs into the mixture, puts it into a greased pan, dusts it with some breadcrumbs and puts it into the oven before going into the café area again. Looking constantly towards the large glass window, thinking how true it is that time moves slower when you are waiting for something. He gets up again, removes the Torta from the oven and returns to the café. His stomach twinges – there she is, turning into the doorway, a blue blouse loosely opened at the neck, coming towards him. With ardent eyes he rushes to meet her, noticing her flushed cheeks and quivering glance, his trembling hands drawing her to the table for two in the window. 'Well,' he bursts out. 'Will you marry me?'

Her voice is soft and her gaze intense as she says slowly. 'Yes, I'm coming with you.'

He immediately begins fishing into a small pocket inside his jacket and takes out a thin silver ring, putting it on her third left finger, holding onto her hand, looking into her beaming face. 'We will be so happy in Italy.'

Vivian twists the ring round on her finger, admiring the small filigree design of curving interwoven threads and then looking up again, asks excitedly, 'Where will we live?'

He strokes the back of her hand. 'Maybe at the family home – it's on three floors with a rickety 16th century wooden staircase in the middle. There's enough space.'

She looks aghast. 'What, live with your parents?'

He scratches his darkly shadowed chin. 'Hmm, maybe not. Uncle Alberto's house by the lake would be better, if it's free'. He jumps up to bring slices of Torta di Riso and coffee and on returning says to her, 'I'll go home in November and sort things out and then you can follow in the spring.'

Her face drops. 'That's a long time away.'

He gently strokes her cheek, 'I know, I know, but it's best not to arrive in winter.'

'Why not?' she asks.

'Because it's very cold then and miserable.' He takes a sip of coffee. 'I'll need to sort things out with Mama and Papa, we can't just begin living together.' He squeezes her hand tightly. 'Don't worry, I'll write to you – it's only three months or so, it'll fly by.'

The little pout disappears, and she says, 'Alright, but only if you promise to take me for a boat ride on the lake.'

'Of course, and we'll dance on the shore, dream in the gorgeous flaming sunsets on Grigna and sleep in the sunshine under the olive trees.' He puts his hand over hers in a possessive curl, 'But first, I'll have to get the priest's permission to marry you.'

Vivian crosses her other hand over his. 'Don't you think you should ask my mother too? It might help her to come to terms with my leaving.'

'Of course, I will.'

★ ★ ★

Vivian, having filled the vase up with water and arranged the Sweet Williams in a pretty shape, enters what used to be Rosie's room to find her mother has dusted the speaker, polished the radio and plumped up the cushions. Vivian notices what a difference it makes to her mother's appearance when she tries. How much younger she looks with her hair washed and put up in a tidy knot. 'You look smart,' observing the crisp white blouse and navy blue skirt and seeing that her mother has even put a little colour on her lips

'Well, it's not often that a visitor comes along. Certainly not a foreign one.'

Vivian smiles uneasily in reply. 'You will be nice to him, won't you?'

Her stomach full of butterflies, she opens the door to a huge bunch of sunflowers which obscure Giulio's face.

She laughs. 'Come in, it's no good hiding behind those.' As she ushers him towards Rosie's room she can see that he has dressed up in his double-breasted, charcoal-grey suit and highly-polished shoes.

He moves towards Vivian's mother. 'I'm Giulio, and I bring you some sunshine from Italy.' With a large smile, he presents the sunflowers.

'Thank you, that's kind,' Vivian's mother says. Ignoring this romantic gesture, she immediately passes the flowers to Vivian. 'Why don't you go and put these in water, dear.'

Looking at Giulio she indicates a chair. 'Do take a seat.' He sits down next to the radio and smiles again, lowering a little briefcase on the floor. 'I understand you have asked my daughter to marry you.'

'Yes, that's right.' He takes his silver cigarette case out of his pocket. 'That's why I'm here today, to introduce myself to you,' he says, offering her a cigarette.

'No thank you, I don't smoke, and I'm afraid I don't allow it in the house either.' Giulio puts the case away in his jacket pocket and, after a small silence, says, 'I'm hoping to put your mind at ease.'

Vivian's mother tips her head slightly in acknowledgement. 'So what made you come to England, then?'

'I wanted to see somewhere outside Italy, so I came via Paris. My Uncle Alberto knows Mr. Fratelli, the owner of Polti's, so I had an introduction. I had an uncle who died fighting alongside the British, so our family loves England.'

'Why don't you stay here with Vivian then?'

Vivian comes in with white lace doilies and lays them out on the table, winking at Giulio as she leaves to get the tea-tray.

'I only have papers until November, so have to go home. Anyway, the winter is always a difficult time. It's cold and my father needs more help these days.'

'Are you the only one then? No brothers or sisters?

'Yes, and I'm the baker, so it's good to have me around.'

Vivian carries in the tray. The sound of pouring tea seems to ease the tension in the room.

'Sugar and milk?' Vivian's mother asks.

'No, just black, please,' he replies, reaching out to take the cup from her hand. Vivian's mother leans forward, putting her elbows on her knees.

'What about Mr Mussolini? Is he a hero of yours?'

'Well, he has done some good things and some bad things. But up where we are, it's different than being in big cities like Milan, Rome or Naples. Life in the countryside still continues in the same old way, more or less.'

'Wouldn't you be better off here, opening your own business in London? After all, that Polti's seems rather popular. You know Vivian can't keep away from it, can you dear?' her mother says, looking at her.

Vivian smiles awkwardly.

'I've thought about it, but it would be hard, and there is already a café that I will own one day waiting for me in Italy. We hold dances in the room on the upper floor, there are delicious fresh fish to eat, you can sail on the lake and ski in the mountains above Mandello.' He bends down and lifts up the briefcase. 'Here, let me show you some pictures.' He passes them to her slowly. 'Here is a ferry crossing the lake on a summer's day and this one is of the café getting ready for a dance.' She studies them closely, without comment. 'Here are my parents, and here are the Grigna Mountains at sunset.' Taking more time over the one with the parents, she nods and gives them back.

Vivian's mother settles back on her chair. 'I see.' Her tone conveys defeat, the logic of his position in relation to the café is unassailable. 'You make it sound and look very inviting, but who would look after Vivian?'

'My family will. They are already looking forward to meeting her,' he says standing up. He goes towards her, and with his most charming smile, says, 'I love your daughter and she will be safe with me.'

As Vivian's mother shows him to the door, he turns to shake her hand. 'Maybe you will come to Italy one day to see for yourself.'

Vivian's mother smiles, looking over his left shoulder 'You never know.'

★ ★ ★

Back in the kitchen, Vivian faces her mother. 'Well, what do you think?'

'I'll give it to you, he's very persuasive. But at the end of the day it's not safe to go to Italy with a man you hardly know. Wait a year and see how you feel then.'

Vivian rests her hands on the back of the chair. 'I see no reason to wait.'

'Don't rush into it.' Her mother puts the tea cups into the sink. 'The passage of time alters things. You might even find you prefer Bill, after all.'

Vivian grips the back of the chair as anger flashes through her. She finds herself shouting. 'You must understand it is not just a matter of preference! Marriage is not just about economic necessity – it must be more than that – ' Her mother turns around and lays her hands down on the table. Vivian lowers her tone. 'I understand what you say and why you say it, but I'm not pregnant. I haven't made, and I am not going to make, the same mistake as you.'

'I'm glad to hear it,' her mother says, with a sorrowful sigh. 'All I can say is, men like Bill don't grow on trees.'

Vivian looks directly into her mother's eyes. 'I love Giulio and I'll take the chance. I will be going.'

★ ★ ★

Vivian has been dreading tonight and, not wanting any maternal interventions, she goes outside the house to wait. Catching sight of him riding his bicycle towards her she immediately feels guilty, knowing the pain she is about to cause. She waves her hand as he cruises up beside her before coming to a halt.

'Hello. Jump on the seat.' Feeling a sense of relief – the sooner they get to the pub the better – she sits sideways and holds onto the back of his jumper as they wobble off down the road. She knows her mother is right, Bill is a nice man who will make someone happy. But not her. The least she can do is tell him now and not wait until it is time to leave or for him to find out some other way.

The evening is still just warm enough to sit at the tables outside. He puts the beers down first and then, taking his jacket off, magics two bags of crisps out of his pockets. 'Hey, got a pay rise today so thought we'd celebrate with two bags. It means I can have a holiday this year.'

'Oh, that's great' Vivian says, taking a sip of beer.

'Thinking of going down to Brighton for a few days. Jack says he'll come too. What about you? Fancy a turn about the pier?'

Vivian takes a gulp of beer and is silent.

'What's the matter, Vivian? Brighton's fun.'

'Bill, I know Brighton is fun but I've got something to tell you.'

'What?'

Unable to meet his eyes, she looks down at his chest. 'I'm going to go away.'

His smile disappears. 'Where to?'

'I've met someone else.'

His mouth drops open. 'Are you saying we're over?'

'It wasn't intentional. It just happened.'

Raising an eyebrow ironically he leans forward. 'So, how long ago did this "just happen"?'

'We first met about six months ago. He's Italian.'

'Oh, that's nice. So you've been stringing me along for six months?' Bill raises his voice. 'Two-timing me with a greasy Eyetie.'

'No, it's not like that,' she says sharply, looking at him directly for the first time. 'He's asked me to marry him.'

Bill is quiet for a moment and then, shocking her, puts his hand firmly on hers. 'But we've been going out for two years.' Leaning forward towards her uncomfortable face he says, 'You know I love you.'

Vivian looks at the tabletop, away from his pleading eyes.

'I've been saving money so I can ask you to marry me.'

'I'm sorry, I can't.' She bites her lip.

'I know we can be happy together, just like Rosie and Jimmy.' A sharp line creases his forehead. 'You hardly know this man.'

'I've agreed to go to Italy soon.'

He flings her hand away. 'You must be mad, going to live in a place you've never even been to. Don't you realise it's full of Rudolph Valentinos and tinpot Mussolinis?'

'I'm so sorry.'

'How can you be sure this is what you want?'

'I've never felt like this before.'

Knocking over the half-finished beer on the table, he grabs her arm. 'How can you do this to me?'

The beer drips down onto her shoes as she pulls her arm free and cries, 'Because I must.'

He looks at her in disbelief.

'Bill, I didn't mean to hurt you, but I can't help it.'

Standing up, he snatches up his jacket, and with a rigid jaw and angry eyes marches over to his bicycle and pedals away.

★ ★ ★

Deep under the blankets, Vivian is sleeping, dreaming vaguely of a house in some woods, enveloped in a garland of sweet almond blossom, beside a dripping lake. She turns over and floats on, a boat is slipping away from her, someone is shouting. 'Don't go, don't go.' First it is a man's voice and then it's her own. Her voice, as she wakes in a start and moans, 'Oh no, gone, he's gone.' Autumn has slid into winter, it's all naked trees, icy starlight and absence now. She runs her fingertips over the sheets towards the slim blue tie he left behind, folding it against her cheek, curling towards it, the woody smell of his cigarette is still there, intermingling with stale after-shave. How time is wearing away at his image, smudging his eyes and blurring the contours of his lips. If it wasn't for the ring on her finger, the brief blurring memories of moments spent together, the slim blue tie and the letter beside the bed, she would think it all but a mirage. She recalls standing beside the Austin 7 outside his flat for the last time. It was packed to the gills, suitcases filling the back seat, shoes on the floor, a map on the passenger seat and a hip flask; remembers saying, 'Surely I can squeeze in, I don't need much.' But he was adamant. Coming round he held her close, wiping the tears away, as he said, 'I'll write to you with all the wedding plans.' She recalls clutching his arm, her fingernails digging into the coarse twill of his overcoat, 'Oh, take me with you now – it's so far away.' She could feel his small, surprisingly strong hand determinedly prising her fingers away as he said.

'My darling, we've been through this so many times. It's too soon, things must be sorted out in advance.' He kissed her gently. 'Don't worry, sweetheart, I'll be dreaming of March and the springtime and you. Trust me, I love you.'

★ ★ ★

Ricca, Carlo's mother, closes the history book and places it on the desk with a sigh. Today it is all about the grandeur of Rome and tomorrow it will be about the Renaissance. Above her desk, hanging side-by-side, are the portraits of King Victor Emmanuel III and black-shirted Benito Mussolini, whose bullet-head is encased in a black helmet. His square-jawed face maintains a sturdy gaze on their eight-year old heads as they all stand up, knowing that the eyes of Il Duce are upon each and every one of them. They can already cite the Fascist Creed by heart, since it is written on a poster on the wall. They understand that Rome is the Eternal City, that Mussolini is a genius and that the Empire will be resurrected.

Ricca stands up to face the children, raises her right hand and they all shout out 'Credere! Obbedire! Combattere!' Believe! Obey! Fight! 'Mussolini ha sempre regione!' Mussolini is always right! before rushing out of the room into the light of day. Each child has been warned that even asking 'why' is equivalent to disobedience when they are given an order. A child who is disobedient is like a bayonet made of milk: their first duty is always to obey. They are taught that Rome the Eternal is reborn not in the nineteenth century but in Mussolini's Italy, and ascended into heaven in the glorious years of 1918 and 1922. In a mockery of the Bible, they recite that they believe in the genius of Mussolini, in the Holy Father Fascism, in the communion of its martyrs, in the conversion of Italians, and in the resurrection of the Roman Empire.

★ ★ ★

31st January 1932
London

My darling Giulio,

I'm so excited that Father Colazzo has at last got permission from the Pope to let you marry me, a mere non-Catholic, and that the date is set. So long as I don't tell mother, Uncle Douglas has given me some money towards my ticket so I've nearly got enough. I've already bought two suitcases and hope that by end of February I'll be able to buy the wedding dress – Mother has agreed to help me even though she wants me not to go.

It sounds good that you're working with Papa in the café and I can't wait to help with all those parties and dances that go on in the reception upstairs. I do have a request for the band to play at least one English dancing song at the wedding reception, otherwise I'm sure I'll love all the tunes you've chosen. Uncle Alberto's house down by the lake sounds very exciting to me and I can't wait to see it. I've got a Teach-Yourself Italian book and can say lots of things – like 'bread', 'milk' and 'please can you help me I'm lost'.

Mason's is as boring as ever. I'll tell them I'm leaving soon but not until I've bought my ticket. Polti's is not the same without the Torta Grigna and Fatty has left and gone to live in Brighton I'm told. I'm still going there every Saturday though, to pretend I'm already in Italy with you because I'm in love with both of you!

Ti adoro, Vivian

\* \* \*

The old porter, breath rasping in his chest, flops the two suitcases down beside Vivian. 'Where are you going, lassie?'

'To Milan,' she replies.

'Alright, follow me, then'.

Vivian watches as he labels the big brown suitcase up for Milan before lugging it along the platform and chucking it into the special luggage van attached to the rear of the train. Vivian, hanging onto her favourite little black leather suitcase with royal blue lining, turns to her mother. 'I'll go and find the seat, then.'

Her mother hands her a little tin. 'Here you are, dear, some Marmite and cucumber sandwiches for the journey.' Like a small child setting off for school, Vivian takes them whilst her mother looks at her searchingly, seeking some recognition of the enormity of the occasion. 'Wish you weren't going, dear. What shall I do without you?'

As Vivian looks down at the floral decorations painted on the little tin, those old familiar waves of guilt begin washing over her – how could she leave her mother alone like this after all she has been through, all that struggle to feed and clothe her? Yet she feels like a caged bird trembling on the edge of the open door, glad that these difficult months of confinement are over. The silences, the air of betrayal and disappointment, and the quiet nights alone are finished. She can't look directly at her mother, but puts her arms around her. 'I'm so sorry, I have to go, it's my chance of something better.' She squeezes those disappointed shoulders. 'I do love you – but I must, I really must – ' Her chest feels tight as she steels herself to turn away and enter the carriage.

Before putting her little suitcase in the netting overhead rack, she undoes the two catches, takes out the Baedeker and puts it on the seat, next to the sandwiches. Letting the window down, leaning out, she grasps her mother's outstretched hand just as the guard blows his whistle. Spitting engine valves hiss, fluffy wisps of steam float up as she kisses those calloused fingers before letting go, waving to the beloved, tearful face as it shrinks away until it is completely out of sight. Struggling with the lump in her throat, she lurches down to the lavatory, shutting herself in and sobbing into her handkerchief until it is sopping wet. Finally, calming down and composing herself, she returns to her seat, keeping her head down to hide her puffy eyes. On opening up her Baedeker she turns to the page marked 'Milan', the pages shaking with the train as she tries to focus on her destination and calm her fearful, excited heart.

# Italy
## March 1932 to June 1940

The train is entering the outskirts of Milan, so Vivian, after a rather fruitless freshening-up exercise in the dirty washing area, dots some Chanel No. 5 on her pulse points and pulls the clean blue blouse over her head — the same one she was wearing when she said 'yes' to Giulio. The whistle screeching and echoing off the cavernous roof of Milan Centrale station makes the butterflies in her stomach flutter ever faster. The grand arching iron-and-glass canopy of Platform 3 comes into view, magnifying the hiss of slowing pistons as the train pulls up before the white painted wooden buffer, exhaling steam from its nostrils like a shining black stallion at the end of a race. Reaching up into the netting, she removes her small black leather suitcase before jumping over the large two-stepped gap between the train and the platform. Glancing anxiously from left to right, she spots him at last under the clock, leaning against the studded steel pillar. She had forgotten how smart he was compared to the English boys: in a felt Borsalino Fedora hat, a white handkerchief sticking out of the breast pocket of a black woollen winter coat. He is smiling, waving a *Corriere della Serra* newspaper. Her heart beats wildly so that she feels breathless and her stomach starts racing as he moves towards her. He's here, he's really here.

He sweeps her up in his arms, bruising her lips with a passionate kiss and then pushing her back. 'Here you are, as beautiful as I remember'.

She moves to him and they hold each other, swaying slowly from side to side before he releases her and takes the big suitcase in his left hand. His arm around her back and she leaning in close, they move slowly down the platform.

'Shall we have a drink before we set off?' he asks.

She looks proudly up at him. 'Oh, I'd love one. Something warm, please.'

Descending the grandiose staircase and stepping out of the portico, Vivian finds herself screwing her eyes up against the sharp early spring light. The pale blue sky is streaked with cirrus clouds as though a painter has brushed a thin layer of whitewash over it, and water is spewing out of the mouths of the two giant-headed fountains, sparkling across the beige limestone. On looking up at the muscular Herculean figures standing at the top of the immense building, restraining two colossal Pegasus horses, she is unable to refrain from gasping, 'God! This building is enormous.'

'It's built to impress. The only small things around here are the people,' Giulio replies, as they turn into Piazza Duca D'Aosta, crossing the tram tracks.

Vivian squeals with delight when they stop at a gleaming black Fiat 514 saloon car. Its glistening upper-lip-shaped bumper seems to be smiling at her. 'What happened to the little Austin 7?'

'It packed up just after the Swiss border.' Giulio swings his arm towards the car. 'This beauty is Uncle Alberto's.'

'I've arrived,' she thinks, admiring the thoroughly waxed beige leather upholstery, noting the spotless ashtrays and catching a distorted glimpse of herself in one of the two large front lamps that shine like mirrors – 'I really have arrived!'

After loading the suitcases, he touches her elbow. 'Come on, let's go over to Caffè Panzera. It's new, opened last year at the same time as the monstrous station.'

The shiny new interior, full of chromium fittings, flashing glass and lacquered wood, is exciting. She sits down near the window and he opposite her. She peeps underneath the three-quarter-length lace curtain at the carvings of military men, lions, eagles, and admires the flags adorning the station. Watching her fascinated gaze, he slides a cigarette into the corner of his mouth and lights up. 'I hope you're not going to be another one falling under the dramatic spell of Il Duce's virile nationalism.'

Vivian laughs. 'That sounds rather high-falutin' – I hope not, too!' She looks down at his hands, then his mouth and finally into his eyes. 'I can't believe this is really happening. I thought this day might never come.'

'I've missed you so,' he says, reaching across to hold the tips of her perfectly manicured fingers. 'You look lovely.' As the waiter approaches with a tray he leans back against the red leather seat.

Vivian takes a sip of her coffee. 'What's the cake-y thing you've got, there?'

'That's a Panettone Ripieno. It's a basic Panettone with a cream filling,' he says cutting a small piece with a pastry fork and offering it to her.

She parts her lips and gently takes it into her mouth. 'Oh – it's much better with cream.'

He smiles, heart in his mouth as he watches her savour the taste, and then eats some himself. 'Did you know that it is called "pane Tone" after a Milanese baker called Tony? It is Tony's Christmas bread.'

She dabs the corner of her mouth with a napkin, laughing.

'No, I didn't. Anyway, how long does it take to get to Man-dello?'

Giulio puts a second sugar into his coffee. 'About an hour and three-quarters.'

'I'm a bit nervous about meeting your mother and father. I bet they'd rather you married a local girl.'

'There's no need to worry, they're dying to meet you. Come on, let's go and put them out of their misery.'

Holding hands, they recross the Piazza Duca D'Aosta. Vivian watches as Giulio puts on his black leather gloves before she settles into her own seat. As he starts the engine, she admires the fine gauges and smooth, shiny steering wheel, and then, once the car is in gear, he turns to look directly into her face. 'Ready for the rest of your life?'

'You bet!' she replies, her eyes agleam as a wild, inexplicable excitement arises within her. She gazes out of the window, eager for the adventure, glancing periodically back at his profile, taking in the strangeness of Milan, floating through the countryside, wanting this dream to go on forever.

★ ★ ★

As his fat, rough hand grazes her long soft fingers, Vivian smiles demurely into Luigi's deep-set brown eyes — they are the same height — while thinking that he doesn't look anything like his son, Giulio. His hair is short, iron-filing stubble, and his chin disappears into his neck.

'Benvenuta, Vivian, come,' he says, pointing to the kitchen and smiling, the gold tips on his two front teeth flashing.

A country man, she decides. Maria, Giulio's mother,

moves forward to embrace her, Vivian bending down so that their bosoms fit together like two pieces of a jigsaw. Maria is stocky, silver threads in her hair, a web of fine wrinkles around her eyes, a shy smile revealing a gap where a side tooth should be. Halfway around the tour of the house, they hear a booming shout.

'Well, where is she, then? Come down, come here, let me look at you, bella Inglese.' Uncle Alberto's tonsure is prominent from her point of view poised at the top of the stairs, his wild eyebrows bushing over laughing eyes as the cigar smoke floats up towards them. She flushes as he runs up lightly, raising one leather knee-length horseman's boot to the step she is on, saying, 'Bella, Bella!' before taking her hand and kissing it, then twirling her under his arm. 'Welcome to Italy, Vivian.' He puffs on the cigar again, vigorously. 'After coffee, get Giulio to come down and I'll show you the new home.' Then, like a passing tornado, he blows out of the door.

Bad weather is beginning to set in, clouds rolling down from the Valtellina, as Vivian and Giulio make the short walk to Alberto's house, Vivian luxuriating in interlacing her fingers through his.

Giulio stops at a prime location: a three-storied house on the corner. 'Here we are.'

Vivian observes that the front of the house faces onto a small piazza, whilst the back overlooks a tiny harbour with small colourful wooden boats pulled up on a stony slope; a black fishing gondola, its tarpaulin rolled up and secured over three hoops, bobs like a cork on the rising waves. 'It really is right beside the lake,' she says excitedly. 'Does Alberto live here?'

Giulio points to his left. 'He has another house further up that hill over there – that's what being a director of an engineering firm does for you.' Then, looking up to the top floor, 'But he stays here sometimes as well.'

The blue shutters are open but the glass windows are shut, dark panes in stark contrast to white, elaborately laced curtains. Vivian makes a mental note to remove the dead plant swinging melancholically from the finely wrought iron balcony just as Alberto steps out of the front door, smiling. 'Go on in, lovebirds, it's open and I'm on my way out.'

Entering through the blue glass-panelled front door, Vivian glances quickly into a small living room on the left of a corridor before moving swiftly to the right, peeking into the two bedrooms off to the left, noting the dark wooden beds. Scooting over the white marble flecked floor, she darts into the kitchen, then whirls back on herself, runs back to Giulio and grabs both his hands in hers. 'It's wonderful, we'll be so happy here.' She pulls him along the corridor. 'Let's have the bigger one as our bedroom.'

He lifts her up and swings her round into the room before clasping her in his arms and pushing her onto the bed. Lying on top of her he kisses her lips, then her ears and neck, before suddenly rolling to the side and stroking her hair. 'I can't stay. They're watching us like hawks.'

'I know, I know,' she sighs, stopping his lips with her fingers.

She follows him to the door and, reluctant to be parted, watches his back hunched-up against the slashing rain now ferociously pounding the cobbles, corduroy trousers soaking up water like a sponge, his lean body weaving around the puddles as he looks back to wave from the corner of the piazza. As he finally disappears she feels the first twinges of nerves and as she turns round to face the musty, empty rooms she finds a shudder shafting down her back. But the next moment, hearing her mother's voice say, 'A grey goose just walked over your grave, dear,' she has to smile, and crosses to the window where the rain-spotted waters of the lake look icy in the fading light, the rough, temperamental wind, the Brevia di Lecco, chopping the surface into white arcs. Little cloud-clumps hang loose near the surface of the water like dirty cotton wool, separated from the dense bank of cloud hanging low on the wooded hills opposite – there seems to be no space between the earth and the sky, no air to breathe. Feeling her momentary confidence drain away again, a wave of fear rises up in her throat and she whispers aloud, 'What *have* I done?' Unable to move, she sees a ferryboat taking its windshaken course across the lake. She can only turn away with a sense of relief when she sees it make it to the other shore.

Looking into the gloomy room, she wonders why the sun always seems to be somewhere else, before turning around sharply. Pursing her lips, she banishes such negative thoughts from her mind, and places some wood on the stove. She undoes her little black suitcase and puts the Baedeker on the bed before opening up the other suitcase. Carefully unfolding her wedding dress, she smooths the creases and hangs it up before unpacking the rest. Finding crockery in the kitchen cupboard, she makes herself a cup of coffee and eats a biscotti, feeling comforted as she looks through the wedding itinerary Giulio has left with her. But still, when she goes to bed that night, the dark wooden bed feels distinctly like a coffin and she is aware that there are no stars in the sky. She lies, acutely alone, listening to the strange sounds of the lake, to rough waves beating the shoreline, to a wild animal screeching, to a footstep on the cobbles, to a creak in the floorboards – a stranger alone in a foreign land with foreign sounds, and only travel-book dreams to cling to.

★ ★ ★

Vivian holds onto Giulio's arm tightly as they walk up the Via del Fosso into the small Piazza San Lorenzo. 'I was afraid last night, after you'd gone – it felt so lonely.'

Putting his arm round her shoulders, hugging her to him, he begins to reply, 'Only a few days to go and we'll be together forever,' but his voice is drowned out by the huge campanile bells tolling the hour.

Vivian, covering her ears, looks up at the tall 12th century tower before they step over the cobbles towards an ornately studded large set of wooden doors. Giulio turns the brass grip handle and steps through the small inset door onto old grey flagstones worn to a slippery lustre by the feet of the faithful. After following him through another set of darker wooden doors Vivian enters the crepuscular, aromatic world of the Catholic Church, this lily-perfumed atmosphere of suffering assailing her senses for the first time. Her eyes are caught by an illuminated painting of a stooping Virgin Mary, so blue and submissive, the orangey red of her halo a small sign of warmth amongst the cold stone and hard wooden pews.

A side door creaks as a robed, dark figure steps heavily into the main body of the church. This must be Father Renzo

Colazzo, holding his hand out to Giulio and leaning towards Vivian, looking into her eyes, putting his right arm around her shoulders, guiding her in towards the darkness, speaking softly. 'It's very good you are here. Giulio has told me all about you and London.'

Gradually, her eyes adjust themselves and she begins to see him better, the white bristled head almost entirely shaven, making his face seem fatter than it is, then the few pale bristles peeking out of his arched nostrils, followed by small pert lips. He is smiling, his dark, flitting eyes looking down as he begins reaching into his cassock, round a small belly, supported by a black belt. Out of the pocket he pulls a set of blood-red translucent beads: a rosary, and, his left hand squeezing her arm, places them in her right hand.

'These are for you, my child.' His voice dripping like honey. 'You must learn to love them.'

On moving into the cross-shaped nave, Vivian stares at the lines on the big expanse of black and white chequered floor, feeling a little dizzy as they shift around in a geometric dance. Looking upwards at the painted ceiling above the minstrel gallery steadies her head. Father Colazzo guides them into the Presbytery on the other side of the nave before turning to Vivian, his honeyed words becoming more impassioned and lyrical.

'I know you are not a Catholic, but here in Italy, it's part of our nationality, part of our soul, we are bound together by the Church. We live by it.' Touching her shoulder, he leans forward. 'You will not be allowed to take Holy Communion unless you are baptized, and in order to marry Giulio you must agree that any children you have will be baptized and brought up as Catholics.'

Vivian, noticing the portrait of a Pope above his head, is self-consciously docile in her reply. 'That won't cause me any problems, Father.'

Moving across to a small marble table, he picks up a document before pointing at the portrait. 'That is Pope Pius the XI and this is his Papal Encyclical "Casta Connubi". It makes clear what is expected of a married couple.' Pulling his head up, he clears his throat, his voice more martial this time. 'Being so new here, you won't have heard the popular saying of Il Duce, "War is to the male what children are to the female". Even though this is the opinion of the government, the Church agrees with it. The role of a wife is to be a homemaker, to obey her husband, and to remember marriage is the union of husband and wife for the purpose of the transmission of life. Each life is precious and should not be prevented by contraception or abortion, even though natural processes are acknowledged. Italy is short of children, which is why Il Duce launched the "Battle of the Births" programme.'

The muscles in Vivian's neck are tense. She could do without this lecture. All she wants is to marry the man she loves, not reproduce to save Italy. Looking over at Giulio for reassurance, she sees his eyes are firmly fixed on the floor.

Father Colazzo, relaxing his stance, his voice less pompous, comes towards her holding out his arms. 'Now that's over, Vivian, welcome to Mandello. I'm here to help you in any way I can. Remember, my child, St. Augustine told us that God loves each of us as if there were only one of us and Matthew 10:30 says "but the very hairs of your head are numbered". So if you ever want to be baptized, come to me. I'll always be here for you. Now, come on over to the altar, and let's run through the order of ceremony and your vows.'

That night, again lying alone in her coffin bed, mulling over the day and the delicious ossobuco and risotto Maria had prepared for supper, Vivian doesn't feel so afraid. The calm waters of the lake slopping against the boats, the soft hooting of a night-owl and the distant bark of a dog sound benign, even comforting, and her beloved Giulio is just up the road.

★ ★ ★

Sunday 19th March 1932 is a clear, bright day. Under the azure sky, tussocks of pale primroses cling to the chilly rocks above Mandello, and tiny bright blue periwinkles push through the detritus of winter. Vivian, blinking away small tears, is looking down at Maria pulling the ties of Vivian's waisted, ankle-length white dress around her slender middle, and thinking of her own mother. How brave of her to come and buy the dress with me, knowing she wouldn't be here, desperate for me not to go. She misses her stoical presence. Self-consciously hiding her sweaty palms, she feels her heart thumping. So, here I am, alone on my wedding day, nobody on my side of the church. A wry smile crosses her lips – fancy having nobody of my own to give me away. Maria straightens the three-quarter-length sleeves for her and places the veil on her head – it has a modern look: a tightly-fitting hat in the centre, with a little row of laced flowers across the front, and appears strangely out of place here. Violet eyes looking larger than usual in her pale face, Vivian stands smiling at Maria, this rustic woman, this surrogate mother of quiet intelligence and a warm heart, saying, 'Thank you.' Taking the simple bouquet of pale pink apricot blossom – picked that very morning from the trees above the town – she begins the walk across to the Church of San Lorenzo where everyone will be waiting, Maria holding her hand and whispering, 'Bellissima, bellissima,' passing her over to Luigi, who will lead her up the aisle.

Walking towards Father Colazzo, her eye catches sight of the image of the big Christ on the crucifix hanging over the altar, blood pouring from his side, his feet and hands pierced with brutal nails. The skull and bones of Adam at the foot of the cross seem particularly large. Tearing her eyes away from the gruesome sight, she focuses on Giulio, waiting at the altar bar, in a special dark suit with an apricot flower in the lapel, a starched collar and dark red bow tie, smiling broadly: her very own saviour, she thinks blasphemously, who would soon be hers forever.

And then blinking in the sunlight, dodging dried pasta and rice, holding hands, walking through the small crowd who call out, 'Bravo, bravo,' as the wedding party makes its way across the Piazza Lorenzo, down a narrow alleyway, to Café Lario, where white ribbons dangling from the Pasticceria sign flutter drunkenly in the breeze. Inside, amongst the pale leaves of spring and more apricot blossom nestling in baskets, are the Bomboneria: sugared almonds to symbolise the bitter-sweet of life, in little parcels of ribbon-tied tulle, one for each guest. Vivian, picking up a silky-smooth satin 'buste' bag, stands by a sideboard, smiling for each person who kisses her and puts some money in the little bag before passing on to shake Giulio's hand. Carlo, Giulio's best man, standing at the bottom of the twisting oak stairs, serves a small glass of Amaretti to every guest. Uncle Alberto, beside him, his thinly-striped waistcoat decorated with a brass pocketwatch chain linked to the third button of his jacket, is nearby with Father Colazzo. He slaps the priest heartily on the back, sending cigar ash fluttering over the cassock and onto his own spats.

By the time everyone has filed past her and Vivian gets to the top of the stairs, everyone is sitting down, including the Mayor – now known as a 'Podestà', since Mussolini reorganised the system of comunes – Guido Morante. He is a Mussolini placeman, resplendent in a grand chain of office. His wife, in a sophisticated beaver shoulder-cape, sits next to Father Colazzo. The two long tables, down each side of the room, are aglitter with shiny glasses and polished cutlery glinting in the candlelight, whilst the space in the middle of the room awaits dancing feet. Standing alongside Giulio, at a small table slightly separated from the others, Vivian raises her Amaretto glass, as do they all, in the traditional 'one hundred years' toast. She can't wait for her first taste of the classic perch risotto of Como. Salivating at the sight of the lemon slices tucked in amongst the soft rice she begins lifting the fork slowly to her mouth, lingering over the delicate flesh of the fish, lightly flavoured with the sage and butter in which it has been fried.

'How's the wine, Vivian?' shouts Luigi across the noisy room. 'All the way from Arneis,' he tells his neighbour proudly. Yet another dish, then another, 'Evviva gli Sposi!' interrupts the lunch as once more glasses are raised in a toast to the long lives of the newlyweds.

Appearing in the doorway, Giulio, bow-tie long gone, cigarette dangling from the corner of his mouth, staggers across the room with a massive Torta Grigna saying, 'I know you only married me for my big Torta.' Vivian, throwing her head back, laughing with delight as he puts it down in front of her, jumps up and gives him a full kiss on the lips. It is the perfect time for the Prosecco toast, so everyone lifts their glasses, shouting out 'Evviva, Evviva!', as, together, Vivian and Giulio smash a glass on the edge of the table. All eyes are on the number of pieces, all want to know how many years they will be happy together. All eyes slide away from the eight large, jagged pieces lying on the white tablecloth.

Luigi quickly jumps to his feet calling out. 'A kiss for the bride, a kiss for the bride,' brushing the unsmashed glass pieces out of sight, whilst the sharp-eyed accordionist begins playing lightly as the Torta is sliced up and passed around.

Giulio places his lips close to her ear. 'Don't worry, darling, Italians love superstition. But it's all nonsense.'

Vivian, noticing one woman whisper something to another, aware that all eyes are watching her as a silky-skinned northern woman who is different to them, paler and more reserved, smiles bravely, the bad omen already worming its way into her heart.

At the first notes of their first song, Giulio grabs Vivian's hand and begins swirling and twirling her around in the centre of the dancefloor, making her forget the glass and relive those moments in the Rosemary Branch when they had eyes only for each other. When the violinist puts down his instrument and starts clicking some castanets with his left hand, whilst tapping out a rhythm on the tambourine with his right hand, Giulio lets go of one of Vivian's hands, beckoning others to join them and form a circle for the tarantella. Moving slowly and then ever faster in one direction and then another, a circle of unrestrained dancers whirls around until people begin to drop out breathlessly and a woman takes a tumble. Confident bodies keep on dancing, wild movements and unrestrained laughter fill the room. Vivian, feeling drunk, flops down in a chair, smiling as she watches Uncle Alberto, standing on a table, his hands raised, his eyebrows lifting and falling as he leads the room in a raucous 'O Sole Mio'. Suddenly he stills his melodramatic eyebrows, stoops down to pick up a knife and clinks it against a glass announcing, 'It's time for you two to go,' with a vulgar wink, swaying his hips backwards and forwards, 'to have more fun, eh.' Jumping down, he pulls Giulio by the arm. 'Come on, I've brought something special for you, something for a *real* man.'

Shouts of 'Evviva gli sposi!' chase them down the stairs where Alberto stands beside a cherry red Alfa Romeo Spider sports car, black leather seats polished to a gloss and white satin ribbons tumbling round the two large headlamps. Waves of excitement coursing through her, Vivian steps carefully onto the fancy ridged running board, waving goodbyes as Giulio begins tooting the horn, and they roar off.

★ ★ ★

Piani Resinelli is 1,300 metres above sea level, so warm coats are needed. Going down the lakeside road towards Lecco, people cheer and wave at the newlyweds. Vivian, wondering if this is all really happening, looks down at the wedding ring shining gold on her finger and back again, proprietorially, to her handsome husband. Turning left up to Ballabio is where the zig-zagging ascent to Alberto's little stone house in Roccolo Resinelli begins. Higher and higher, hairpin after hairpin, Vivian saying nervously. 'Be careful, it's icy up here.' Looking at the Grigna peaks, covered in thick snow, ice clustering in the couloirs, Vivian realises they really do look like a Torta Grigna, all dusted with icing sugar.

The drop gets bigger and as the rear wheels slide a bit Giulio catches her eye. 'Don't worry, I know the road. We'll soon be there.'

'Won't it be freezing in the house?' Vivian asks.

'No. Alberto will have had a fire lit and made it all cosy, I'm quite sure.'

Darting in out of the cold as soon as Giulio unlocks the door, Vivian feels herself being lifted up in his arms and carried upstairs, kicks her legs and squeals whilst he whispers words of love on her mouth and neck – and then drops her on the bed, tearing her wedding dress off. He pushes her, unresisting, back, fumbling with his flies, and she gasps when he enters suddenly, unable to delay any longer. Feeling a sudden thrust and a stab of pain, she gives into the rhythmic movement and then the final shudder. Stunned by the brutal encounter, she lies still until he withdraws and rolls onto his back, letting his breath return to normal.

'Is that it, Italian style?'

He turns towards her, gently stroking her breast. 'No, it's just the beginning,' and starts kissing her body all over again, more fervently, her body beginning to soften and relax as he slowly comes back alive.

Drowsing until late in the morning, Vivian feels content, sensual, as she runs her fingers across the flesh of his back, then through his chest hair, letting them run all the way down, and murmurs, 'Let's stay in bed all day.'

'Alright then, but I'm hungry,' Giulio says, throwing a shirt on and disappearing downstairs. He returns, sliding back under the covers, carefully placing a little tray on the end of the bed. 'Here we are then. Bread, some Bitto cheese – that started life in a stone hut on the pastures above Val Monastero, dates all the way from Arabia – and Prosecco, naturally.'

She leans back against the bedhead, sipping luxuriantly from a glass. 'Have you and Carlo known each other forever then?'

'Yes, his mother Ricca is a teacher at the school, where we were together. His father, Giuseppe, works as an accountant at the ammunition factory. They're Jewish, been in Mandello for generations. Carlo's done Bar Mitzvah but they're very relaxed about it all.'

Vivian, recalling his thick black curls, jet-black eyes and thick eyebrows meeting in the middle of an aquiline nose, is thinking, 'Oh yes, he looked Jewish'. 'Doesn't he work at Café Lario?'

'Yes, Papa is giving him work whilst he decides what to do – he wants to be a lawyer but things are too uncertain at the moment.'

'What do you mean?'

'Fascism – you have to be a party member to stand a chance of getting any job. All Professors have to take the Fascist oath.' Jumping up, he clicks his heels together and raises his right arm rigid in front of him. 'Must do the Roman salute – handshakes are bourgeois, apparently.'

Vivian screws up her face. 'Doesn't look right without any trousers or boots on.' The Prosecco has gone straight to her head, as usual, so she leans across, grabbing his legs. 'Come back to bed,' she says, pulling his shirt off and clambering on top of him, feeling brave enough to take the initiative for the first time.

The next day, holding hands they walk through bald trees admiring the catkins and rock-sheltering primulas, tricked into emerging by the pale sunshine. Giulio turns towards her. 'You know, we can come here as much as we want. Alberto never minds.'

'Let's come here a lot, then. I want to try all seasons here.' She waves her arms around expansively. 'It's so... majestic.'

He points to the left. 'See that green over there, near the church? We're going to open a new café right there.'

'Where would the customers come from?'

'A new railway and road are planned – one thing Il Duce is good at – and there's even talk of a ski-lift.'

Vivian clutches his hand and looks up at him with hopeful eyes. 'Please let me help in the café. It'd be so much fun and my Italian will get better. I know it will and I'm sure I'll be good at it.'

He smiles at her. 'You and Carlo then, perfect.'

After a translucent dawn, their last day arrives and they sit on the steps of the church unloading their little basket. Vivian fills the glasses with Vin Santo and begins dipping crisp Cantucci in the mellow amber, whilst Giulio spreads golden honey, made by the hands of Cistercian Monks at the Abbey of Piona on Monte Legnone, onto the bread, and tips it gently into her mouth.

The day turns into a winter-white afternoon as Vivian begins to pack. As she picks up her Baedeker from the table,

Giulio lifts it from her hand.

'What is it with you and that book?'

'I've loved it since I first saw it at Masons. I used it on the train coming here, looking at all the route maps and reading about the places I went through on my way to you.'

He flicks through it, homing in on the Lake Como section, reading aloud: '"at the Punta di Bellagio the SW and SE arms of the lake unite. The latter, the Lago di Lecco (twelve and a half kilometres long), though inferior to the other in picturesqueness and luxuriance of vegetation presents grander mountain scenery. The abrupt E. bank, with its steep sleigh-paths, is skirted by the railway mentioned at p.196."' Flicking through a few more pages, he passes it back with a dismissive gesture. 'This is for dreamy northern tourists.' He swivels towards the door, grinning as he looks back over his shoulder. 'You'll get the real thing with me.'

As she bends her knees to lift her little black leather suitcase into the car, she has a distinct sense that this is the end of the beginning, she will remember this moment as the time when their real life together began. Her eyes survey the latticework of snow that nestles into the crags along the jagged wall of Monte Grigna Meridionale as Giulio puts the gear into first to begin the serpentine run down to the lake. On leaving the serried embankments spread out like green ribbons along the hillsides above Lecco, entering the edge of Mandello, Vivian's eye is drawn towards a surreal sight in a clearing at the edge of a small copse; what can it be? A cluster of schoolgirls of about nine years old, black pleats of school uniform skirts swaying, white tights, white jumpers and white blouses with a sticker of Il Duce's face at the neck. In a commanding voice she says, 'Stop, Giulio, I want to watch.' Music plays slowly over a radio as they cradle dolls in their arms, rhythmically rocking their babies. 'Whatever is going on there, then?' she asks.

'Doll drill – Piccole Italiane, the little girls' section of the Balilla.'

The music stops and a grey-suited man with a white shirt and pale Naples Borsalino hat begins strutting over the grass towards a set of bigger girls, the Giovane. Alongside is a matronly woman, obviously a headmistressy type with long black skirt, white blouse with a black tie and a black beret. The Giovane raise their right arms in the Roman salute, each then picking up a wooden hoop garlanded with ribbons in the national flag's colours of red, white and green. Music starts up again as, under the rigorous gaze of the officials, they undulate and sway, weaving the hoops about in a display of feminine grace. A strange yet familiar feeling begins to creep over Vivian, that same feeling she had at school when Miss Hanley ordered her to find her peg bag. She has always hated that other people always think they know how you should behave, which box you should fit into. And here this kind of control is colourfully visible, displayed in childish games. A claustrophobic, panicked feeling of needing to break out starts to engulf her.

'I think I've seen enough,' Vivian says, with a shiver. 'Let's go.'

'Ah, yes,' sighs Giulio, pulling away. 'Mussolini likes to get them when they're young. Shape them in the Fascist mould.'

\* \* \*

How she loves the café life, where all sorts of people rush in for a rendez-vous, to argue, to escape, to hide, to gossip or simply to pose before leaving again. Normally, Giulio leaves early, without her, but not today. Her eyes are alive with anticipation: it's her first day helping with the baking. Holding hands, they take the short stroll past the lake and then into the nearby Piazza where the three-storey, green-shuttered building stands, tucked into a corner. Café Lario takes up the full width of the building, with its twirling 'Pasticceria' sign straddling the whole of the large double-doored entrance. A warm, enticing glow emanates from the large red and yellow stained-glass light above the doors. Green sash bars, in a ribbed fan arrangement, sprout sculpted metal stems of daisy-like flowers. It reminds her of Café Polti, except more rough-and-ready inside. The big awning announcing SPECIALITA TORTA GRIGNA has been rolled away for the winter, and the small square wooden tables and walnut bistro chairs are still stacked up at the back, under cover.

Giulio pushes the key in deep to unlock the double green wooden doors of Café Lario, throws the keys onto a dark oak bar and flings open the windows to clear the air. 'We'll leave the clearing up to Carlo, let's get straight to it.'

Vivian breathes in the comforting, homely smell of the tidy bakery kitchen for the first time and snatches up one of the voluptuous marrons glaces sitting invitingly on a large tray. 'Sorry, I can't resist.' she says, popping it into her mouth as her eyes survey the contents of the shelving. Pretty, patterned pizelle irons sit waiting for batter to be poured into them and be turned into a lacy snowflake biscuit. Next to them are a variety of metal mixing bowls and a flower-shaped copper baking mould. There are jars of salt, confectioner's sugar, ordinary sugar, cocoa powder, vanilla liqueur, olive oil, almonds, cinnamon, almond essence, anise, hazelnuts, pistachios, rum syrup and, spotting the eye-catching small bright red bottle of cochineal, she picks it up. 'What is this fantastic one for?'

'Funny you should like that one – it's used in Zuppa Inglese. An English trifle.'

Laughing, she puts the cochineal back and glances down at the sacks of chestnuts and sealed bags of flour on the floor and then above at the liqueur bottles. She turns to Giulio with an enquiring look. 'What are these?'

'This clear one is grappa, a pomace brandy distilled from what is left after the grapes have been pressed for wine. It's very strong. This dark golden brown one is Amaretto from nearby Saronno.' He opens the rectangular glass bottle and puts some on a small spoon. 'Try it.' She takes it onto her tongue and wrinkles her nose at its bittersweet almond taste. 'I use it in tiramisu, pancakes, coffee. This other clear one is Maraschino, another bittersweet almond flavour, distilled from cherry pips – an import from Croatia and, finally, this brown one is straightforward Jamaican rum.' He puts his hand on her shoulder. 'Come on, let's get on. I thought we'd start with "sbrisolonia", or "crumbly cake". It's easy and quite common.'

'What's that then?'

'It's a specialty of Lombardy – from the city of Mantua, they say.' He ties a baker's apron around his waist and then hers, pulling her backwards as he pushes himself into her, fondling her breasts, burrowing down into her neck.

She wriggles forward and shifts over to the pastry table. 'Hey, I thought we were supposed to be making a cake.'

He pulls away, whispering, 'But you're so irresistible,' and then, back to a businesslike tone, 'It's a good introduction for you, since it comes from the ingredients of the land. Poor people using what they had: cornflour, lard and hazelnuts. Can you mix up a cup of white flour with some cornmeal? While I put some sugar, ground almonds, a bit of vanilla liqueur, a teaspoon of ground coffee and a pinch of salt in a bowl. We are lucky here in the café, as we have more exciting things to add.'

'Finished,' she says, turning round.

'Here, catch,' he says, throwing a lemon across to her. 'Grate the zest, then we can mix it all together, put it on the pastry board and make a little dip in the middle.'

He chops up some butter and a bit of lard while Vivian separates four egg yolks from their whites. Together they pour the egg yolks in the little dip and begin kneading the doughy mixture, their hands entangling and sticking together. He picks up one of her fingers and licks the dough off.

'Oh, how disgusting, you'll be ill!' Vivian laughs.

When the mixture is safely into the baking-tin they stand with their heads touching as they place the unpeeled almonds in a star shape all over the top.

Vivian puts the cooked sbrisolonia on the counter and bends down to gets some small plates and forks. On hearing a commotion, she looks up to see Uncle Alberto has swept through the door and is looking down at her.

'Ah, bella Inglese. Nice to see you're not afraid to work.' He opens a small wooden box inscribed with 'Toscano'. Lifting a cigar out, he bends his head to light it and she catches its sweet aroma.

'That's lovely, do you always smoke those?' He blows some smoke directly at her.

'Yes, they're the best, handmade in Tuscany.' He clicks his fingers at the sbrisolonia. 'Come on, then, come on! The service is too slow here.'

'Would you like some dessert wine or a cup of hot coffee with it?'

'Excellent, you know the traditions already,' he says chucking her under the chin.

'Hot coffee.'

She flutters her eyelashes. 'Yes, and I made it too.'

'Bravo, bravo. Is Giulio around?'

'Out the back, I'll get him' she says with a charming smile.

Alberto nods to Giulio when he enters, wiping his hands, and they take a seat by the door, leaving Vivian on duty at the counter.

'Things are bad at the factory,' Alberto says. 'I'm having to lay people off and cut wages. Mussolini is putting all the money into armaments.' Alberto spreads his legs expansively. 'I'm sure he's planning to invade somewhere.'

'Well, I had noticed there's a depression going on. The newspapers never stop harping on it.' Giulio lights up his cigarette. 'Supplies are costing more.'

'I don't suppose you can take another person on here? Fabio is supporting the whole family.' Alberto sits up, 'I can recommend him. I've spoken to Luigi and he says it's up to you.'

'Send him in, I can probably find something.'

As Alberto opens the door to leave he looks at Giulio.

'Good. Now, don't you forget: Mussolini is always right. The rumour is, you might think otherwise.'

★ ★ ★

Spring is tardy; the cold, damp mountain winter clinging on until well into April and Vivian is desperate for sun. Finally, in the second week of May, stepping into her frilled swimsuit, she looks back over her shoulder and calls out to Giulio. 'Right, I'm going in'.

He watches her go. 'You must be mad. Nobody swims around here until July'.

Hobbling into the water on feet as tender as a baby's, inching forward over the small stones, she stops, water at her knees, hands on slender hips, sucking in her lips as small, lapping waves creep icily up her thighs. Flaring her nostrils to inhale the sweet, light spring breeze, she tilts her face upwards in worship of the bright afternoon sun. Onno, opposite, no longer looks threatening, as it did on her first night. The cluster of houses hugging the shoreline, nestling under the densely wooded hillside, seems inviting, as the comforting sound of a church bell drifts over on the wind – you are never far away from a church bell in Italy, she thinks. What would her mother say if she could see her now? Perhaps she would understand the beauty of it all and forgive her for leaving. But probably not.

The snowy peaks of the Valtellina are visible in clear skies, and to her left the shoreline on both sides of the lake bends inwards like a protective arm, enfolding her in its comforting embrace. A flash of sun on a window in Onno reflects onto the lake, creating a tapering silver shimmering pathway like a stairway to heaven, drawing her in. Spurred on by a dipping duck nearby, she takes the plunge. A shuddering moment of searing iciness, followed by instant numbness. A small crowd has gathered on the shore, clapping and shouting 'Bravo, bravo, Inglese' as she swims out through little fronds of vegetation and startled fishes. She knows she is a figure of interest to them: another pallid northern tourist, but unusually one that seems to have come to stay rather than simply pass through. Turning back to the shore, a seal-headed dark figure cutting through the glistening twinkles of light that dance on the lake, she looks up at the rugged limestone rockface of the Grigna Mountains towering over Mandello, and realises that, even though she doesn't have any close friends, this place is beginning to feel like home.

Giulio wraps a towel around her goose-pimpled body and then encircles her in his warm arms. They hear a buzzing sound, and turn around as it gets louder to see a yellow float-plane descend onto the lake, its landing struts, like ducks' feet, outstretched towards the water, and tail-light aglow. A white spume of spray accompanies the revving of the engine before it lifts off again, banking to the left like a monstrous butterfly in search of nectar. Vivan nestles back into Giulio's arms, feeling safe and secure, sure that she has become one of God's chosen people.

★ ★ ★

Mandello-del-Lario,
30<sup>th</sup> June 1932

Dearest Mother,

I am writing to let you know that all is well here, that at last the warm weather has arrived and I have had a swim in the lake. I am practising my baking skills as I am now allowed to help in the café. It's such fun, like being in Polti's all the time. Giulio always promised me a boat trip to Villa Melzi and yesterday my dream came true. We took the lovely old white paddlesteamer 'Concordia' up to Bellagio. The fine mist of morning lifted and the lake was like a piece of glass so that the white three storey palace looked like a huge wedding cake reflected in a mirror. We wandered round the ornamental lake and down avenues of plane trees looking at statues and temples. The owner was a good friend of Napoleon apparently and lots of famous people have stayed in the Villa. Masons seems a million light years away now and I'm beginning to feel at home here. I do think of you and miss you and it would be nice to receive your news.

With love,
Vivian

★ ★ ★

Giulio unlocks the double green doors of Café Lario and amidst the smell of stale tobacco sets about cleaning the nickel-plated coffee machine, banging the base of the grinders against the edge of metal bins to loosen the dregs of yesterday. Hearing a motorbike pull up outside, engine left running, he looks up as Carlo Tandini strides in. 'Just checking that tomorrow is still on.'

'Yes, the guns are clean.'

'Right, where shall we go?' Carlo takes an imaginary aim.

'What about the old favourite: Zucco della Rocca – I'll pick you up at eight outside your house.'

'Bene. Ciao,' Carlo replies, and dashes out of the door.

Giulio watches the lithe figure, almost feline in its grace, flit onto the bike and glide away, realising how private his friend is. Cerebral, an only child like Giulio himself – maybe that's why he feels like Carlo's big brother, despite their being roughly the same age.

The next day, Giulio checks through the eight different-sized pockets of the hunting jacket before pulling on his brown cloth trousers. He attaches a 12-round cartridge holder onto the oiled leather belt, picks up his shotgun and goes outside to his beloved Guzzi Normale. After putting the gun in a slot at the side of the bike, cocking his leg over the shiny pale tan leather seat and jerking the starter pedal, he revs off. Easing the bike into the side of the road, he watches the dust swirl around Carlo's feet as he walks towards him, fits his shotgun alongside his, sits on the rack at the rear of the bike and puts his legs up on the struts at the side. Grabbing onto Giulio's leather-jacketed back, Carlo shouts, 'Let's go!' his curls dancing along the wind as they skid off up over the railway line onto the winding road to Maggiana. Leaving the bike by the washing fountain in Piazza Fontana, they make their way up through the paths snaking around the backs of houses, past small garden plots with drooping tomato plants and old wooden chairs set under the shade of olive trees: on they go, up through little vineyards shored up by crumbling drystone walls, their luscious grapes already plucked, until finally they enter the mottled light of the woods burnished in autumn browns and golds.

Here, amongst the birch, beech, oak, conifer, chestnut and ash, they clamber over small rocks, not talking, staying still for half an hour or so at a time, falling leaves drifting onto their backs, shotguns cocked, eyes like stalking tigers. A screech pierces the silence, the undergrowth rustles and a vivid red eyelid flashes.

'MINE!' shouts Giulio, standing up and firing. A black grouse, flapping its panicking wings, rises up into the air. Another shot cracks out as the bird flops back into the bushes. 'No, mine,' says Carlo with a winning smile, before picking it up and putting it into a small sack.

Carlo may have had the first blood, but by the time they get up to Zucco della Rocca, two partridges with feet strung together hang over Giulio's belt. Climbing to the top of the rock, the primitive satisfaction of a kill coursing through his veins, Giulio looks down on the lake before dropping the dead birds on the ground, open beaks and fixed eyes facing the sky. He sits down under a low branch as Carlo opens his rucksack and tosses out Robiola and Taleggio cheeses, plus a few tomatoes and olive oil in a little wood-topped jar.

Giulio uncorks the red wine and breaks the bread in half. 'Hunting makes you hungry.' He picks up a piece of cheese and asks, 'Seen Giovanni Farace recently?'

Carlo picks up some bread. 'Saw him down at the Dopolavoro the other day, drunk, strutting about like a heel-clicking moron in front of the fourteen-year-olds standing there in their silly knickerbocker Avanguardisti uniforms and blackshirts.'

'Why do you go down there then?'

'It's only 10 lire a year and if you want to play football or anything they run all the games. There's skiing trips and discounts at theatres in Milan.' Carlo scrapes the earth from underneath his nails with the point of a knife. 'You should join.'

'What and spend time with idiots like Giovanni Farace?' Giulio sneers. 'You must be joking.'

'They're not all idiots. There's a Marelli radio down there

so you can hear the latest.'

Giulio, looking down through the dizzy rocks to the gleaming lake, sucks his teeth.

'Yes, but why would I want to listen to two-hour official broadcasts of Benito Mussolini, eh?'

'Don't be so pig-headed, you should listen for your own sake, keep in the know – it's always good to stay on the right side of history.'

Down in the pasture below the rock, Giulio ties some string around the hind legs of the two dead hares they've just shot and latches them over the right handlebar of the bike, their ears dangling just in front of his right ankle, clots of congealing blood already settling on his trouser leg. Carlo fixes the grouse over his left shoulder, hangs the partridges over the other handlebar and hops on the back.

Just as they are about to set off Giulio glances at him. 'I'd rather be a pig than a sheep – anyway, who says Mussolini is on the right side of history?' He shoots the bike away so quickly that Carlo has to grab onto the back of his jacket to stay on board.

★ ★ ★

The front door of the three-storey house is open. Giulio goes down the side of the large 16th century wooden staircase, into the big kitchen where his mother sits chopping parsley at the old wooden table. Laurel and olive wood are burning in the old stove and strings of onions dangle enticingly above two pots worn from use. The raw smell of dead flesh enters the room with him as he greets her, 'Mama,' throwing the kill down on the table. 'Here's a couple of birds and a hare for you. Where's Papa?'

'In the café – he wants to talk to you about old Pepe's do next week'. Maria pokes at the stiffening haunches of the hare. 'I'll make a salami with this. It'll marinate overnight. Pass me the sharp skinning knife from the drawer, would you.' As he hands her the knife, she lets out a small sigh. 'Papa's tired, he needs help. Maybe you can take over, gradually.' She turns her troubled eyes towards him. 'With the biscuit factory gone, he's spending more and more time worrying about the café. Everything costs too much. It's difficult making ends meet.'

Giulio puts his hand on her shoulder. 'I know. Don't you start worrying, as well.'

★ ★ ★

January 1933 is full of freshly fallen snow, softly waiting for the heavy footprint of man. Her stomach churning with excitement, Vivian pulls her gaze from the edge up to the sharp serrated crags of Monte Grigna cutting into the ice-blue sky like knives, as they snake up the icy road to Alberto's little stone house in Resinelli once more. Her stout laced boots are tight, but she feels agile in the sleek black ski slacks and tightly-waisted matching black skiing jacket.

'I shall fly like an arrow,' she says to Giulio, who is waxing the solid wooden skis. Picking her pair up, she puts them over her right shoulder, takes the poles and starts trudging up the path to the slope behind the Church of the Sacred Heart. At the top she slides her boots into the ties, pulls the leather straps up round the front and tells him she's ready. Coming up

MARA G. FOX

behind her, grabbing her in his arms, he nuzzles her hair and whispers, 'I'll guide you down, just relax.' He is an impatient teacher, but fortunately she is a fast learner, so parallel turns come quickly, and soon she sets off alone; Giulio laughing and chasing her down the slope where she falls over, snow in her hair, he tumbling into her. Lying together in the soft powder, under confetti snowflakes falling glittering from the trees, as if under a spell, she catches his right hand and kisses it over and over again, whispering, 'I love you, I love you. ' After struggling up, she stuffs a snowball down his khaki jacket and sets off up the hill again, splaying her skis in herringbone style.

'You will be a good skier by the end of winter,' Giulio says, overtaking her.

★ ★ ★

'It's bitter today, but then it always is for February Carnevale,' says Carlo as he serves shots of strong coffee in small cups to two men standing at the bar.

Through the hazy smoke, Vivian can see four men at a back table playing cards – she has begun to realise that the Italian café, unlike the English, is primarily a masculine place. The band arrives, and a dust-coated violinist strikes a note as the rehearsal begins, followed shortly after by a group of three people with masks and painted faces, followed by the Mayor wrapped in a flag. Shouting children parade along the lakeside banging drums and eating fried dough ribbons called 'gossips'. Roberto Maletti, who has been preening around the bar for some time now, orders two more grappa, whilst his brother,

Marcello, removes his Tyrolean peaked cap (of the $2^{nd}$ Alpini Regiment) and runs his right thumb and forefinger along its black crow's feather, arching his left eyebrow and giving Vivian a knowing wink.

'You look smart,' Vivian says, flushing as she thinks how handsome the brothers are, so sharp-edged with their short hair and leather belts; different from when they hung around the main Piazza, unemployed, hard-headed and threatening.

Roberto, reaching into the pocket of his pristine grey-green military jacket, ostentatiously retrieves a five lira note and slams it down on the bar. 'Due birra.'

Vivian notices a little tremor in Giulio's jaw as he asks caustically. 'You going to drink all your wages? That's your fifth.'

Marcello replies breezily. 'Yep, 20 lire a day for camping and skiing in the mountains, no rent – why not?'

Without a smile Giulio replies. 'Because that's cheap, for cannon fodder.'

Roberto, his voice becoming steely, fixes his eyes hard on Giulio. 'An army marches on its stomach and we get more food than we can eat.'

Giulio snorts.

'They're even naming a mountain after Mussolini so you can run up and down that in your uniforms.'

Vivian glances up at Giulio's sneering face. Recently she has begun to notice a sarcastic side to him. It's increasing, and she doesn't like it. Seeking to defuse the rising tension, she kicks the side of his foot. 'Don't be mean – they look lovely,' smiling sweetly as she passes the Maletti brothers their change. As they walk away, shoulders softening, jaws relaxing, Vivian leans towards Giulio. 'Why make trouble?'

'They're idiots, that's why. They've no idea what they've got into.'

★ ★ ★

'We want to sing of the love of danger, the habit of energy and rashness. The essential elements of our poetry will be courage, audacity and revolt.
[...] We want to exalt movements of aggression, feverish sleeplessness, the double march, the perilous leap, the slap and the blow with the fist.'

> *– Filippo Tommaso Marinetti*
> *'The Futurist Manifesto', 1909*

Getting ready for her first trip to Milan since her arrival, Vivian checks her red lipstick in the mirror and settles her new silk scarf into her neck , wondering that such a luxury is quite normal here, given all the silk factories around the lake. Raring to go, she puffs her curls up into a looser shape. It must all be so sophisticated down there. She can barely contain her excitement. While changing trains, Vivian doesn't notice the drawing of helmet-headed Mussolini in a square-jawed, belligerent pose, and the militant graffiti: 'BELIEVE, OBEY AND FIGHT' no longer surprises, having subsided into the obscurity of the familiar. The whistle blows and Vivian beams at Carlo sitting opposite Giulio, dressed smartly for the occasion, pensive and all in blue. But as the train pulls out of Lecco Station, two blackshirted militia men stand up, revolvers at their belts, and stride menacingly through the carriage, eyeing up the passengers. 'What on earth are they doing on the train?' she whispers.

'Oh, they're National Militia men travelling free, enjoying the glamour of the uniform,' responds Carlo. 'It's the 28th October, the 11th commemoration day for the March on Rome in 1922, so there'll be more than usual, going up for the parade.'

Giulio waves his right arm in the air dismissively. 'It's a myth, there was no march on Rome – Il Duce caught the night train south from Milan.'

Vivian nudges him in the ribs. 'Ssh, you'll attract unwanted attention.'

Into the teeming morass that is Milan Central Station they plunge – flags, uniforms, guns, dogs, musical instruments, jewellery, fine hats and laughter surround them whilst the public announcement system plays a medley of Fascist marching songs. Outside in the Piazza Duca D'Aosta, the little white fridge on wheels belonging to the gelati seller is surrounded by squealing children despite the nip in the air, and the sweet kiosk is awash with customers. Dodging cyclists, they cross the Piazza diagonally to Café Panzera and sit down outside under the cosy awning amid aromatic laurels.

Vivian pulls the red silk scarf tight into her neck against the growing chill of the evening breeze and leans towards Carlo. 'What exactly is it we are going to see?'

'*Simultanina* by Marinetti – I don't know what it's about, but Marinetti is famous for his Futurist Movement.'

The waiter brings dark pink Campari and sodas, putting the heavy-bottomed tumblers down carefully on the white tablecloth, alongside tomato and basil crostini.

Carlo continues, 'People love his plays, they like to go and get offended.'

Giulio leans forward and takes a crostini. 'They put glue on seats sometimes so that people get stuck in them and damage is done to the theatre as well as the clothes.'

Vivian lifts the wheel of orange out of her glass and sucks it before taking a refreshing sip of the bittersweet Campari, listening attentively to Giulio.

'Also, two tickets are often sold for the same seat just to ensure, in true Fascist style, a fight happens. He even introduces heckling at his own shows.'

Looking forward to the craziness of it all and wondering what she has let herself in for, Vivian is enthusiastic. 'I can't wait.'

The theatre is festooned with a colourful array of posters, mainly in red, with big black block letters saying 'FUTURISM' and 'SIMULTANINA – a divertimento futurista in sixteen syntheses'. Inside, to the right, Vivian sees a little dining area with wooden chairs and marble-topped tables.

'Come on,' beckons Carlo, 'let's have a little snack before the show.' They sit down and Giulio raises his left hand, beginning to read in an exaggerated fashion from a printed card stuck in the middle of the table. '"Eating futuristically, one uses all the five senses: touch, taste, smell, sight and hearing – every dish will thus be preceded by a perfume attached to it." – Marinetti, 1930.'

'What's on the menu?' Vivian asks.

'The tactile vegetable garden, apparently,' Giulio replies in an ironic tone.

'You don't have to do this, you know,' Carlo says, looking at him.

A waiter with a massive swirling moustache, a black shirt and white gloves approaches them with a small pink tray carrying a perfume spray in a glass bottle. He places it in the middle of the table and, with a flourish of his left arm, puts before each of them a plate of cooked and raw green vegetables, without dressing. 'Tuck in.'

'Any knives and forks?' queries Carlo.

'No – just use your mouths,' replies the waiter with an inane smile.

'What, no hands?' asks Giulio.

The waiter smirks, 'No just your faces.' He spreads his fingers of his right hand towards them and in rising glissando voice says, 'Feel the food on your face and lips.' Vivian watches Carlo plunge his face in first, followed by Giulio and then does the same. A stick of carrot goes straight up her nose, peppery spinach leaves tingle her lips and dry mushrooms cling to her palate before she comes up for air and to chew only to find herself facing the end of a nozzle in the hand of the waiter as a cold perfume of rose and mint tickles her skin. She sees Carlo, trying hard, looking serious, concentrating on chewing despite being sprayed whilst Giulio spits bits of hard cabbage out onto the table, waving the white gloves away, snorting at how ridiculous it is. Enjoying the nonsense, she dips her head down again to continue the unique dining experience.

Vivian is still fairly hungry when she follows Giulio into the noisy, sweaty theatre. It is three-quarters full, right up to the red velveted top tiers, and she notices she is one of the few women there, confirming her growing awareness that the

the Professor's trousers,' she says and laughs as they turn the corner. It is so quick, so unexpected, finding them standing abreast like the three musketeers, lurking in the shadows. Gallo in the middle, pumped up and jutting his jaw forward. 'Come on, you little bastard,' he says, edging towards Carlo, his upper lip drawn back baring his teeth. 'Come on, you little piece of shit.'

Vivian hears a click, smells alcohol, sees the stiletto switch-blade shoot out, its vicious edge flashing. Her heart leaps as Carlo squares up to him, twisting to the right as the blade skims under his left rib, catching his skin, staining his pale blue shirt red. He spins round to catch Gallo's right arm, enabling Giulio to kick the knife out of his hand before clutching the open black shirt, tearing it back and pushing his face down into the gutter, shouting, 'FASCIST SCUM, FASCIST SCUM.' The other two musketeers come snarling out of the shadows, punching at Giulio and Carlo, and giving Vivian enough time to pick up the knife. Fear spurring her on, she waves it around her head, shouting, 'BASTA, BASTA,' attracting a crowd who begin to form a circle around them. She screams as a drunken man lunges forward, his filthy hands pawing at her breast and grabbing her around the waist; her dress tears as she turns to fling the knife away across the road where it skitters over the slimy surface, spinning and twisting under a parked car. Giulio punches the man aside, clutches her right wrist and barges his way through the milling throng. He drags her up a side street, 'Come on, come on,' as her scarf slips from her neck and is trampled under foot. Gallo, having struggled to his feet, sees them go and stumbles towards them, spitting out on his white breath. 'Your time will come. You will pay.'

★ ★ ★

Vivian sits, listening to the rhythm of the train wheels. Aware of the adrenaline still coursing through her veins, she notices her hands are trembling slightly. How could a night out at the theatre end like this, in a street brawl? Her eyes have been opened tonight. The veneer of civilisation has cracked open and something deeply unpleasant has made its way to the surface. Vivian looks across at Carlo, quiet and pale in his blood-encrusted shirt, melancholy, intellectual eyes studiously trained on the Simultanina programme. She interrupts him. 'What is it between you and Giovanni? Why does he hate you?'

'It's all because I broke his nose, made him look a loser in front of his friends.'

Her brow furrows. 'But he wanted to kill you tonight.'

Carlo raises his fist. 'He's a blackshirt. For him, to be a man you have to spill blood.' Giulio turns away from his reflection in the window, towards her. 'It's not just that. You see there is history between Papa and Giovanni's Papa, who is a Fascist of the first hour.'

Vivian tilts her head to one side. 'Meaning?'

'Meaning, one of the earliest followers of Mussolini. As a local party member he kept trying to enforce petty regulations on the biscuit factory – Papa resisted for as long as he could, but in the end he had no choice but to do as he was told. Then came the hungry years, costs rose, wages cut, strikes followed and the factory closed.' He sighs. 'It broke his heart.' Giulio looks back to the window. 'There will always be bad blood between Giovanni Farace and us'.

The train wheels grind on as Carlo's cigarette lighter grates in the silence between them. 'You see, Italy has always been a land of feuds. This is just another one.' Carlo blows out a smoke ring that floats aimlessly across the carriage.

★ ★ ★

Vivian dresses with care today, putting on her brand new beige-framed sunglasses, even though the sun hasn't come out. She pulls her pastel blue skirt straight and steps outside, her mouth aflame with lipstick. How kind Alberto is to lend them the Alfa Romeo sports car for their second wedding anniversary. Giulio is already in the driving seat, resting his elbow nonchalantly on the side of the open window.

He smiles. 'OK Como, here we come!'

She gets in. 'How many times have you been to Como?'

'Oh, lots. We'll go down the lakeside to Lecco, over the bridge at Malgrate and go across inland until we reach Como.'

'And have you been on the funicular before?'

'Yes, once. Papa had a cousin who lived in Brunate and we went for lunch. You'll love it.'

After driving down Viale Lecco they park by Piazza Matteoti and begin their stroll around the lakeside towards Villa Olmo. The sunlight comes and goes on the surface of the lake, as, holding hands, they join the other promenaders. Vivian quite enjoys being looked at and is beginning to be able to stand the heat of appraisal she receives in Italy. She knows her violet eyes, pale skin and auburn hair mark her out as exotic and different, and she half-likes the flagrant Italian male gaze which makes no secret of its brazen intentions. She also knows that she is regarded as Giulio's possession and that's the way it is. She doesn't mind. Giulio is different, and a cut above them, anyway.

On the return to Como, they stop to see the red, green and white of a Caproni CA 100 Idro floatplane begin its descent towards the landing stage. 'See, they're the colours of the Italian flag,' Giulio says.

'You don't say,' she replies sarcastically. The Aero Club Como flag flutters in the wind as the whirring sound of the front propeller gets louder. Watching a plane land on water seems so dangerous, so exciting, that Vivian grips Giulio's hand and holds her breathe until touchdown. They have to weave through the noisy crowd waiting for the next ferry. Expensive little suitcases, smart suits and chic scarves distinguish the visitors up from Milan from the locals. Vivian glances at the small carts packed with vegetables, crockery, saucepans and cheeses. A chicken clucks in a crate as the ragged child beside it crunches the shell of a hot chestnut in her teeth. At Piazza Alcide they enter the little cabin of the funicular and float up through the old Commune of Brunate to what seems like the top of the world. The flag of Italy flaps and the wind whistles past Vivian's ears as she looks down at the small white horses on the waters of the lake, and Giulio points out to her the tiny dot that is Villa Olmo.

Back down in Como, and after a walk round the interior of the ornate Como Cathedral, they take a seat at a café in the Piazza del Popolo. Vivan orders her favourite, a Campari and soda, whilst Giulio has a shaken Negroni.

Picking up an olive with a stick, she asks, 'What is that half-finished building over there?'

'It's the Casa del Fascio. Mussolini's new project.'

Vivian admires the sleek, rational lines already visible. 'It's going to be big.'

'That's the idea. It's going to be the headquarters of the local branch of the Fascist Party, a testament to their power. They want to know the latest news on every street, so they can control us all and lock up those who don't believe.' He takes another sip of his drink. 'It may look like a monument to rationality and the age of reason, but it relies on the primitive. It's like an octopus spreading its tentacles.'

'Oh well, best to keep a low profile then,' Vivian replies, spitting out an olive stone and looking across at the other café, where two blackshirts swig from their Peroni bottles, perusing the piazza with faces even more fearsome than their Neapolitan Mastiff dog.

At Torno, Giulio pulls the Alfa Romeo over to the side of the lake and switches off the engine. As the sun sets, he leans over and gives her a long and intense kiss.

★ ★ ★

She now realises how terrible it must have been for her mother. It's bad enough with a husband, but to go through this all alone? Vivian chews on a piece of bread for temporary relief but nothing seems to take the taste of bile away for long. No more helping in the café, the smoke makes it worse. Her world has become shrunken, nauseous and yellow. She closes her eyes and tries to conjure up a picture of her mother's face, but only fragments appear, never a full image. To escape the four walls she pulls her coat on and drags herself up the hill to visit Maria. Pushing open the door, she hears voices, and bursts into the kitchen to find Giulio tucking into bread and salami at the table.

'Oh, sneaking home to have lunch, then, instead of seeing your poor sick wife?'

'Just brought some flour and butter up for Mama,' Giulio replies, soothing ruffled feathers with a sweet smile as he gets up, kisses her forehead, and leaves.

Gradually the nausea lessens but Vivian spends much of the winter lying down, being kicked from within, watching her body expand until her navel sticks out and waiting for Giulio to come home with café news. She feels stranded, out of things, unprepared.

★ ★ ★

Looking down at the small head lolling backwards, sated and sleeping, she moves the baby into a massive black pram and walks slowly outside to a small wooden table, where the writing pad awaits. Gazing out across the dazzling water, she muses on how strange it is that pain is instantly forgotten once it is over. All she recalls now is how she scratched and clung onto the arms of Mariella, the midwife, as she screamed, enveloped in an ever-escalating world of pain. She remembers the sweat and tears once the brutality of birth was over and her small, slippery baby was placed on her stomach. She can still see the pride in Giulio's eyes when he first saw his son, how he cradled him gently in his arms, kissing his forehead. She picks up a pen, dips it into the ink and leans towards the page:

Mandello-del-Lario
25<sup>th</sup> May 1935

Dearest Mother,

I am sitting outside my front door in the warm sunshine with your beautiful grandson, Leonardo, fast asleep in his pram. He has a full head of dark hair, bright blue eyes and is eating like a horse. I'm toying with the idea of going for a short walk along the beautiful lakeside as am gradually feeling stronger each day. The birth was long and a shock – I guess the first time is always a surprise – and of course nobody tells you how awful it is. I am beginning to realise that having a child changes your life forever and means saying goodbye to your youth. A girl who is the daughter of some good friends of Giulio's family – Concetta Galli – is coming in each day to help around the house and I'm glad of the company and Giulio's mother, Maria, pops in but she is not feeling very well lately. She gets out of breath and her heart is beating too fast.

Giulio is kept very busy with Café Lario and this will be the first full summer of the Café in Resinelli so I will spend the hottest days up in the mountains where I have a friend called Francesca – she has two sons so I can learn from her.

I don't really think it will be possible for me to get over to see you until Leonardo is much bigger and realise it is far too difficult for you to come here so am sending you a photograph of him and will send you others.

Please give my love to Uncle Douglas and here is my love to you.

Vivian

★ ★ ★

Vivian smiles at Maria as she pulls down the edge of Leonardo's flowing blue christening gown, wondering how on earth she would have coped without her. Maria has taught her everything; how to bathe him, how to hold him and how to encourage him to take the nipple. Now here she is today, a new mother with her breasts full of milk and her heart full of love. Since custom requires that whoever brings the child to the baptism must carry him on the right arm if a boy, or the left arm if a girl, Maria nestles Leonardo into the crook of Luigi's right elbow. She looks at him sternly. 'Remember, if he is to be strong and brave you musn't look behind as we walk to the church.' At the end of the Mass, Father Colazzo invites Giulio, Vivian and the godparents, Ma and Pa Galli, to the font. He leans the baby backwards and pours water on his head three times, intoning, 'I baptise thee in the name of the Father, the Son, and the Holy Spirit.' Ma and Pa Galli agree to keep the light of faith burning brightly in Leonardo and as they leave the church, sugared almonds are thrown to the small crowd of people who have gathered outside.

The reception room above Café Lario is decked out with blue ribbons and the sweet smell of lily of the valley permeates the air. Trestle tables covered in white tablecloths line the edges of the room, glasses glint in the sunbeams, pastry forks glisten, the Bomboneria await in baskets, and the Prosecco chills. Several of Giulio's angel cakes, dusted with icing sugar and full of the lightness of egg whites, stand at methodical intervals along the tables. The violinist and accordianist are playing an 'Ave Maria' as the guests climb the stairs and blowing in through the window, a light early summer breeze rustles Vivian's hair. She watches the bald head of the Mayor, Guido Morante, approaching. Towering over her, he lifts her right hand, bends his head and purses his voluptuous lips, letting them linger on the back of her hand. His almond-shaped eyes leer with suggestion as he brushes his fingers across the side of her breast, as if by accident.

'Congratulations on being a new Mama.' She feels relieved as he moves away, over towards Carlo. As the band gets louder, Uncle Alberto grabs Vivian by the arm.

'First dance for me, then!' as he twirls her under his sweaty armpit, before pulling her up close to him and then swaying her back again as he calls out, 'Ah, bella Inglhese, bella Mama.' His brass pocketwatch chain jingles and her face lights up with pleasure as he twists her round, telling her loudly how pretty she is today. He swirls her about until she is dizzy and then passes her over to Carlo, who steadies her as Alberto sashays over to join Guido Morante and Giulio.

Alberto addresses Guido directly. 'Not dancing today, then?'

Guido's bald pate shines like a mirror as he bends his head to the left, saying sardonically. 'Not yet.'

Alberto lights up a Toscano cigar. 'I hear that you were on Lake Maggiore in April at the same time as the bigwigs.' He raises his eyebrows expectantly.

'Yes, I was there. Il Duce looked magnificent in his grey uniform and black shirt. He put on quite a show at Stresa Station. The band played the 'Marseillaise' for the French and then later 'God Save the King' for Ramsay MacDonald, followed by 'Giovenezza' each time.'

Alberto waves the cigar about in front of his paunch. 'Did you get to the conference yourself?'

'No it was all very secretive. Stresa was jam-packed with soldiers, the Grand Hotel out of bounds and important guests were whisked around by motorboat.'

'What was the meeting about, do you know?' Giulio enquires.

Guido looks down imperiously at Giulio. 'The Stresa Agreement of course. Il Duce is committed to Austrian independence but Hitler wants Anschluss. The French and English want to maintain a common front with us against Germany.'

Alberto flicks his ash around. 'Thank God Mussolini is proving to be such a master statesman!'

'Good news, for a change,' Giulio says as he waltzes off to take his beautiful wife in his arms.

★ ★ ★

MARA G. FOX

'The anti-Pacifist spirit is carried even into the life of the individual: the proud motto of the Squadrista: 'Me ne Frego' (I don't give a toss) written on the bandage of the wound, is an act of philosophy not only stoic, the summary of a doctrine not only political – it is the education to combat, the acceptance of risks which combat implies and a new way of life for Italy. Thus the fascist accepts life and loves it.'

– *Benito Mussolini, The Political and Social Doctrine of Fascism (1932)*

The 2nd October 1935 does not start well. Leonardo wakes up early in the morning – far too early, but Vivian is so excited about the trip she doesn't mind. However, Giulio does. Word has gone round that there is to be another balcony speech from the Palazzo Venezia in Rome, Mussolini's favourite platform, and they are going to have a family day out to the main Piazza in Lecco to listen. Looking across the room at Giulio's scowling face, she risks broaching the subject of the trip. 'I'm really looking forward to this, aren't you?'

Banging his coffee cup down on the table, he grunts. 'No.'

'Oh, why not? It'll be my first time.'

'It'll be about Ethiopia, probably a declaration of war. I can't stand it – watching the crowd being led by the nose like a flock of sheep.'

Vivian crosses the room, takes his hand and looks at him with soft, pleading eyes. 'Please come, it'll be our first day out since Leonardo was born.'

He turns his face away. 'No, you go alone. I'll take Leonardo around to Mama.'

'Will you be cross if I go?' she asks.

Leaving the room he calls back, 'No, I know it's just theatre for you, so enjoy it.'

The crowd in Lecco Square are in festive mood, Vivian can feel the buzz of excitement as church bells ring and fluttering Italian flags flash red, white and green in the autumn sun. Trumpet-shaped Radio Marinelli speakers hang from posts in clusters of six, children jostle around the ice cream man, office workers in suits, women in smart hats and labourers in flat caps mill around whilst old friends stand gossiping. Above the noise she hears the sound of an off-tune marching band coming closer. Vivian turns her head to the corner by the church, just behind the Alessandro Manzoni statue, where a band of fifty testosterone-fuelled Fascisti come marching into the square in lines of ten, rifles on their right shoulders, swaying their left arms and snapping their heads left and right as they sing:

| | |
|---|---|
| *Me ne frego* | I don't give a damn |
| *de la galera* | if I end in jail |
| *camica nera* | the blackshirts |
| *trionfera* | shall prevail |

Letting her eyes rest on the brilliantined curls of Giovanni Farace, she takes in the large silver buckle on his black leather belt and the tight shoulder strap crossing his chest from a right epaulette. The tassel on his black fez swings to and fro, close to the Fascist symbol as his knee-length glistening black boots ring out a martial beat on the stones. Small boys run alongside them waving pennants and shouting 'Evviva L'Italia! Evviva Il Duce!' as they pull up in front of the swaggering Mayor, standing beneath a placard emblazoned with a picture of the Empire-builder himself, Il Duce. Feeling fearful suddenly, she ducks her head amongst the crowd, not wanting Giovanni to notice her. A priest parades across the piazza surrounded by altar boys holding up images of saints, dogs bark, and sturdy, dark Fascist Party officials stand about in all-male groups, looking about them all the time as daylight begins to fade.

The Marinelli speakers crackle into life and 'Giovenezza' blares out, followed by silence. The night air is filled with electric expectation as waiting faces are lit up in the glow of flaming torches. Then a tidal wave of sound bursts from the speakers as the roar of the Roman crowd swells to fill the square in Lecco – 'DUCE! DUCE! DUCE!' Mussolini's bark bursts forth. 'Blackshirts of the revolution! Men and women of all Italy! Italians spread throughout the world, beyond the mountains and beyond the seas! Hear me!' The crowd are momentarily silent. 'A solemn hour is about to sound in the history of the fatherland. At this moment twenty million men and women occupy the public squares of all Italy. Never in the history of mankind has there been a more gigantic spectacle.' The Roman crowd roar again, and his voice rises. Vivian feels the hairs on the back of her neck stand up. 'Twenty million men, one heart alone, one will alone, one decision...' She glances furtively at the enraptured faces around her. 'It is not only an army that strives... but a whole people of forty-four million souls, against whom an attempt is being made to consummate the blackest of injustices – that of depriving us of some small place in the sun...' Pausing for effect, and rolling his Rs, he controls the current of the crowd's blood. He is shouting now. 'With Ethiopia we have been patient for forty years! It is time to say enough!' The masses in Rome cry out 'ENOUGH! ENOUGH!' as the man next to her, mouth open, spittle settling on his bristling moustache, pumps the air with his fists, shouting wildly 'BASTA! BASTA!' his voice mingling with all the others around her. Feeling the thrill of the moment, the thrusting dynamic of war, she looks at the spellbound faces of the women nearby as they wait to be swept away, noticing one woman's fingers clutching at her breast, the brutal maleness of Mussolini tapping into her secret fantasies. Il Duce's voice, hoarse with emotion, flies into a crescendo. 'Italy, proletarian and Fascist Italy of Vittorio Veneto and of the blackshirt Revolution, on your feet! Let the cry of your decision fill the heavens... a cry of justice, a cry of victory.' The whole square erupts again, flags are waving, hats are thrown up into the smoke-laden air as the people chant 'DUCE! DUCE! DUCE!' – and in the energizing thrill of the moment she lets herself go, allows herself the pleasure of joining in the drama of Italy, raising her fist and shouting 'DUCE! DUCE! DUCE!'

Vivian slips out of the square, afraid that she might be identified as a foreigner, one of those who have denied Italy its small place in the colonial sun. As she makes her way to the station she still feels electrified, excited and yet ashamed all at the same time. She knows that she has not only witnessed the populace surrender their souls to the magnetic showman, but she has colluded with them, been a willing participant in mass hysteria. She decides not to tell Giulio what she has done.

★ ★ ★

On the 6<sup>th</sup> May 1936 Giulio throws a copy of the *Corriere Della Sera* down on the table in front of her. 'There you are, the fruits of your day out.'

She reads the massive headline.

### STORICO ANNUNCIO DEL DUCE
La guerra e finita,
L'Etiopia e italiana.

She looks up. 'It's what the people wanted. Ethiopia is theirs.'

Giulio moves to the window, gazing out. 'Maybe, but they're ignorant, driven here and there by their master, the pedlar of dreams, the new Roman emperor.' He swings round towards the sink to grab a saucepan lid, puts it on his head and stands on a chair to give the speech from the balcony. He raises his voice, sticks his chin out and rolls his eyes. 'Believe me, I'm the new Augustus. Obey me, Giovenezza! Giovenezza! Give me your youth. Give me your springtime. Come and fight with me and die in a foreign desert.'

Vivian is still laughing as he steps down and comes closer to her, lifting her chin with his forefinger, his voice severe.

'Now, you wouldn't be one of those silly women swooning with delight over Il Duce, would you?'

★ ★ ★

Vivian places the small bottle of olive oil at the bottom of the cloth bag, next to the bread, wine, water, tomatoes, glasses, salt and two lemons. 'Come on,' she says to Leonardo as she tugs at the little white hat she has put on his head to protect him from the late August sun. 1937 is proving to be a hot one, so they've left it until early evening before venturing out. She hands Leonardo a fishing net with a wooden handle. 'Here, let's go and catch some fish with Papa today.' Leonardo grabs hold of it and runs squealing towards the water as Giulio drags the little rowing boat down the stony ground and into the lake. Vivian lifts Leonardo over to Giulio, hands over the bag of supplies and hauls herself over the edge of the boat, making it lean heavily.

'There's no need to sink us,' Giulio says taking up a steadying stance. He takes his shirt off, grabs hold of both oars and rows out onto the lake, turning northwards, up towards Olcio.

Vivian leans back. 'This is so lovely,' she says, admiring his sculpted body and watching his tanned muscles ripple as he builds up a rhythmic pace on the oars. Leonardo hums with happiness as he drags his hand through the water, creating a small white wake in the languid lake.

They moor up near the edge, just by a rocky outcrop on the shoreline. 'The summer is not a favourite time for the trout, so they like to hang around under the rocks to keep cool,' Giulio says, as they all disembark. 'You take Leonardo for a swim further down and I'll try and catch one.' He stands with the water up to his knees, bends down and puts his hands down. It is a waiting game but eventually a trout passes through the gap between his hands and like a flash he grasps it and pulls it up, throwing it onto the rocks where it thrashes about until death comes. Vivian fillets the trout with a small sharp knife, leaving the skin on and removing the grey flesh as instructed, whilst Giulio and Leonardo gather some twigs and leaves to make a barbecue. He puts a bit of wire over the flames, sprinkles some oil on the fish and after crushing a cut lemon with his fist, pours it over the trout.

Vivian gazes at the fire. 'Why don't you want us to go down to Milan?'

He flips the trout over and removes the blackened skin. 'Because it's not safe.'

'Why not?'

'It's got worse since we saw the Marinetti.' He squeezes more lemon onto the fish before putting it back on the wire. 'I heard that the son of a friend of Alberto's, Bernardo, went down to the Piazza Repubblica. Somebody started singing the Socialist hymn, the Internationale'. He flips the fish over so that the skinned side is down. 'A passing Fascist squadistri heard it and entered the square arresting Bernardo, amongst others.' He puts the golden fish onto a plate and slices it up. 'Here, let's eat.' Vivian dips some bread into the oil, places a tomato and slice of fish on top, and puts it into Leonardo's mouth before eating some herself. 'And Bernardo found himself under a bright, naked lightbulb saying he knew nothing. As a consequence he was invited to drink two glasses of castor oil as a toast to the Patria and thrown out of the door to vomit, and worse, in the street.'

'Surely he was just unlucky?'

'Yes, he was just in the wrong place at the wrong time. Milan is where it all started for Mussolini and it is absolutely full of his henchmen. There is no need to go there, unless of course you have to.'

Vivian clinks her glass of wine against his. 'You have persuaded me.'

★ ★ ★

It is February, a cold day, and it seems as though the winter of 1937-8 will never end. Vivian is tired, lying like a beached whale on a sofa near the wood stove. She hasn't felt so sick this time but her back is truly aching. The baby has got hiccoughs so she massages her swollen abdomen murmuring, 'Nearly there, nearly there.' A crash makes her start, the door flies open and Giulio rushes in. 'What on earth is it?' she asks, looking into red eyes in a face drained of all colour.

'It's Mama, she's... she's... dead.'

'Oh my God, how?' She struggles up to hold him. 'When?'

'In the kitchen, a heart attack. Papa found her on the floor: too late to say goodbye.' Tears begin streaming down his face as he looks up at her. 'This winter was just too much for her.' Thinking that seeing a man cry is one of the saddest things, she squeezes his hand. He strokes her stomach, mumbling. 'Now she'll never see this one.'

Vivian doesn't stay long after the burial. Her ankles are swollen by all the standing, and so much crying has worn her out. She lies down and listens to the clock ticking, wondering if this baby will be a girl; after all, she can relax now that Italian honour has been satisfied and Giulio's virility verified by the birth of a son. She thinks about mothers – her own tough mother, tough out of necessity and now without her daughter nearby. Then there was soft and gentle Maria, gone from her son forever; yes, it would be lovely to have a daughter. She sits up, her thoughts interrupted by voices in the corridor. She

123

recognises the robust tones of Alberto.

'Your father can't do it any more, he's worn out, and now heartbroken.' She hears a boot being thrown down. 'Carlo's a good man, get on with it.'

'I know, I know,' Giulio replies agitatedly. 'But all that 'autarky' business, Italy being self-sufficient and all that, hasn't worked. Sanctions make it harder, everything is more expensive. You know that yourself.' Another boot hits the floor. 'It's the foreign adventures. Mussolini would rather spend money supporting Franco in Spain than feed us here. It's all about the army and grandstanding around the Mediterranean.'

'Well, have you joined then?'

'What, you mean join the army?' Giulio snorts.

'No, signed the Fascio Book. Don't look like that, you need to – it's the way to get your hands on stuff.' Alberto's voice softens. 'Look, many people don't believe Mussolini is always right. Remember the Sicilian proverb. "Bend over, reed, and let the tide pass you by." Why give the likes of Giovanni Farace the pleasure of denying you – ah. I see you don't know yet. Well, he's the boss down in Lecco now, policing the agricultural supplies, getting rich.'

'Never,' comes Giulio's quick reply. 'I will *never* become a meal-ticket fascist.'

Alberto is growling now. 'If you sign the book you'll get the supplies. You don't have to go anywhere near Farace for that to happen.'

'And you don't think Farace's spies won't tell him?'

'Why give him the anti-fascist stick to beat you with? You don't have to do much to get arrested these days. Just do yourself a favour and sign up.'

'You might be hand in glove with them. I've seen you drinking with them. I suppose that's how you get your "stuff" for the company, sucking up to them. Well, not me.'

Alberto's steps are on the stairs as he bellows behind him, 'Think of the children, for a change!' Vivian shuts her eyes. The walls seem to be closing in on her.

A week later, the midwife places Emilio in her arms, his eyes wide open and staring into hers with that special intensity of the newborn, unleashing that unique flow of love between mother and child. She kisses his head. Here he is, born on the cusp of spring and yet in the shadow of war and death.

★ ★ ★

Resinelli
21ˢᵗ July 1938

Dearest Mother,

I am up here in the mountains nursing Emilio. As you will see from the photograph he has gone completely bald which is just as well for the summer months. I think he looks a bit like Leonardo but with less pointy features, although I know it is early days yet. Giulio won't let me help in the café anymore so I am lucky that Francesca is so welcoming. She and her boys take us frog hunting and if we are lucky we can barbecue the legs or fry them with some oil and tomatoes.

Things in Italy are a bit difficult on the food front at the moment but we are luckier than city people because we are closer to nature. I am sorry to say that Giulio's mother died just before Emilio was born – a heart attack. We all miss her and Giulio's father is heartbroken. It means that Giulio has completely taken over the running of the cafés so he is very busy and luckily has lots of support from his friend Carlo. I am missing you and would love to receive a letter from home.

With love,
Vivian

★ ★ ★

Vivian begins to get ready to go out, knowing that as another winter looms, life can only get harder. Emilio is starting to crawl, Leonardo's still not old enough for school and there is no Maria to help any more. She calls to Leonardo. 'Come on, let's go and see Ricca.'

'No, don't want to,' he says, puckering his lips.

Thank God for Concetta Galli, she thinks; how precious it is to get time off for a swim or a walk in the woods. 'Come on, put your shoes on.'

'No, they've got holes in them,' Leonardo whines.

How she misses working in the café, even though Giulio tells her that it's not fun any more since all people want to talk about is the Civil War in Spain and how many Italian soldiers are being sent there to fight for Franco. 'Never mind, Leonardo, it's not raining,' she says. 'So come on.'

Ricca lets her in, and Carlo immediately whisks Leonardo

off to play football in the garden. 'Here you are, a fine cup of roasted barley coffee for you,' she says with an ironic smile.

Vivian throws off her shoes. 'I'm going to miss the real stuff, and, more seriously Giulio says there's talk of cafés having to shut early because there's no coffee coming through, just the surrogato.'

Ricca's ample bosom rests on her knees as she looks sympathetically across the table. 'That's probably down in the cities, surely not here.'

Vivian, as quick as a flash, responds knowingly, 'Oh yes. There's a thriving black market going on down in Milan.'

Ricca's shiny gold bracelets on her wrist jangles as she stubs a cigarette out on a tin lid and reaches out her arms. 'Here, give him to me.'

As she jiggles Emilio up and down on her knees Vivian notices that there are dark rings visible under Ricca's coal black eyes and asks. 'How are things with you?'

'I've just lost my job.'

'But you've been there for years. Why?'

'The school has been told, no Jews on the premises. They don't want Italians being taught by Jews. It's been building up slowly, but now it's getting worse. They've even introduced books with titles such as *Little Carl, the Vengeful Jew* and *Get After the Jews*.'

'That's horrible.'

'It's ever since Italy got into bed with Germany. It's not a balanced love affair. Hitler is calling all the shots.' Ricca wipes her eyes with the back of her hand, leaving smudges. 'It'll be Giuseppe next – no Jews in any professions and certainly nothing military.'

'But has anyone ever said anything to you, you know; anything nasty?'

Ricca unfurls Emilio's chubby fingers from her necklace. 'No. In fact most of the other teachers are upset.'

'But how will you all live?'

'I'll try and get some work teaching the Jewish children who can't go to school any more. There aren't that many though.' She looks down at the little whorl on the top of Emilio's head and says in a reflective tone. 'Poor Giuseppe will just have to grow more vegetables.'

'Things are getting worse, aren't they.'

'Yes, these days you can't question anything – the value of the lira, the power of the Italian army or the health of Il Duce.' Ricca gets up and switches on the radio. 'There, now we can talk properly without fear of being snooped on. The latest I've heard is that Mussolini has special staff who go through letters from adoring women, selecting a special few for a private audience. If they take his eye, he launches into them; either on the floor or on a window seat overlooking the Piazza Venezia. Many an interview finishes on the carpet.'

'It can't be true, surely.'

'There's even a rumour that an artist left with not only a portrait but with a child.'

Vivian laughs as she takes Emilio back and gives him her bent right thumb to chew on to ease the teething pain.

Ricca continues. 'Mussolini spends hours in that Palazzo Venezia worrying about the Roman traffic police summer uniform and whether people are reading English or American books, whilst the army goes to pot.'

A flash of realisation goes through Vivian's mind. 'I

haven't received a letter from my mother for ages. Do you think they're being stopped?'

'Probably being opened and read down in Lecco, so they never even make it up here. It's Regime paranoia.'

Vivian hauls a wriggling and squirming Emilio up on to her right hip. 'Let's go outside.' They walk into the garden where the mature sun's last light picks out a ripe, red, unreachable apple suspended at the end of an arching branch. A solitary bee optimistically probes the few flowers, dying and pale, as Ricca looks into Vivian's sombre eyes.

'It's getting nastier and nastier,' and then, putting her hand on Emilio's soft pale curls, 'I fear for us all now.'

★ ★ ★

Winter passes, and April comes again. Apple tree buds are blossoming into flowers. Olive trees, shooting out their pale silvery leaves, glisten in the sun, and the freshness of spring still thrills the air. Vine leaves are escaping from twisted, knuckled wood to trail over arches in the small Arcadian side terrace where, on a roughly-hewn wooden table, a simple lunch is set out. Giulio knows how much Luigi finds comfort here in this little hillside home on the edge of Mandello, near the mule track to Resinelli where he and Maria spent so much time together. He notices scrawny old Pa Galli pat his father on the shoulder, then pass him a glass of beer – the unspoken thread of friendship holding down the years. Leaning back against an olive tree, enjoying this rural idyll, he feels the sunwarmed rough ribs of the bark massage his back as he watches Vivian stroll through the cottage garden where tomatoes, courgettes, beans and leeks will grow. She dips her hand in the water-bucket set under a little stream, bending to take an ice-cold crystal sip. He lights a cigarette and inhales – her waist has thickened a little, but she still looks slender in her pale blue cotton dress. He still wants her. She is not the decorative-needlework type of woman; and yet, all the same, he just wishes she wouldn't keep bringing the children round to the café all the time. He fell in love with her because she is different, the restless type that is unafraid to take chances but she can't expect to be treated differently to the other wives just because she is English. He can't protect her from the expectations of others. She needs to settle down and be a mother. He waves to Leonardo, who is ascending a rope ladder, swinging about before beginning his climb into the apple tree, and laughs at Emilio stumbling around engaging in the fruitless chase of hens through the tall meadow grass. He gets up and walks towards the pony trap, calling out to Luigi. 'Hey, let's go and get the sack'.

Lunch is over and Emilio sleeps peacefully under a blanket, but the wind is getting up as the sky darkens over Mount Megna on the opposite shore of the lake. Off to the right, a large bank of solid black cloud is creeping down from the north like a sheet of armour bearing down on them.

Giulio jumps up. 'Alright, I've got a surprise for you all – come on, Papa, help me, then.' They lift it up onto the table and he rips off the greasy piece of string. Like Aphrodite arising from the sea, the glossy wood and silver knobs of the Phillips radio slowly emerges from the grimy grain sack.

'What a beauty,' says Pa Galli, fondling the glittering fretwork. 'How did you get it?'

Giulio switches it on. 'Old Pietro, the scrap man – this was the last one of three he just got his hands on.' He starts twiddling the knobs. 'Let's see if we can get Radio Londra.'

Vivian puts her hand on his arm. 'Not out here! You know it's Italian channels only – do you want us all to be arrested?'

He pushes her arm aside. 'Why don't you help clear away the plates, and stop interfering?'

Pa Galli intervenes. 'She's right, you know. Informers are everywhere.'

Giulio curls his lip dismissively. 'Everybody knows you need a radio. Now that we have signed the Pact of Steel and Germany is at war with Great Britain and France, it's just a matter of time before the war comes home. This'll be a lifeline for us, you'll see.'

'Yes, but it's not here yet,' snaps Vivian, standing with arms folded, watching Giulio reluctantly wrap the radio up as one would a delicate child, and put it back in the trap.

\* \* \*

Having pulled the empty suitcase out from beneath the seat, Giulio steps down off the train. Quickly moving through Milano Centrale Station, he leaves through a side doorway, avoiding the posse of armed police threatening the grand entrance. There is nothing written down, all he knows is to meet a man called Andrea in the botanical gardens behind the Palazzo Brera.

Even the bright spring day cannot remove the atmosphere of menace as he walks down the Corso Venezia. The anti-British and anti-French posters plastered on doorways are graphic representations of Blackshirts breaking the chains that tie Britain to Gibraltar and Suez, and a pistol representing the French in Tunisia is pointed at the heart of Sicily. At the end of the Corso, there are two more. One shows John Bull and the American Goddess of Liberty astride a juggernaut, riding all over the poor people of Europe. The other shows the pair at a cannibal banquet, eating the corpses of other European countries. Cutting through Piazza Duomo, he finds himself in the midst of a demonstration. Students and Blackshirts are carrying a coffin draped with the British and French flags. Standing at the edge of the largely silent crowd that has gathered to watch, he can see some students are carrying figurines representing France and England as lovers. Holding them aloft, they shout obscenities. The other students put the coffin down and set both flags alight as the Fascist squadistri throw their clubs onto the blaze to make it even bigger.

Glad to get away, he takes the quickest route to the botanical gardens and, after hiding his suitcase under a spreading tree, starts ambling around, examining the vegetation. Soon he notices a short, square man with a prominent belly, aged about 40, standing with a small suitcase, next to the spreading tree. He strolls over. 'Andrea, by any chance?'

Andrea has a look of avarice mixed with anxiety. 'Yes, yes. Let's be quick.' He snaps open the suitcase lid so that the 30 bags of sugar can be seen.

'Thank you,' Giulio says, handing over a wad of money. 'My suitcase is over there.'

Sitting on the train, his hands feel clammy. Supposing the Fascist Militia decide to search this line today. Given that sugar is limited to 500g a person per month, it'll be obvious what has happened. Whilst Andrea seems safe, how can anybody guarantee that he wouldn't, under torture, name Father Co-lazzo as the go-between? If he, Giulio, gets home in one piece, there is no way he is going to tell Vivian about what he has been doing – she can go on thinking he was at work as usual. He goes straight to the café, round the back of the stairs and hides Andrea's suitcase inside a small cupboard, behind a stack of chairs, before going home. As soon as he opens the door, Vivian is ready with the ambush.

'I've been looking for you, where have you been?'

'At work, as usual,' he replies, sitting down heavily and lighting a cigarette.

'Well, it's unusual for you to wear a suit to work.'

He blows a smoke ring at her. 'What is this, some sort of interrogation?'

Vivian waves it away. 'Look, Ricca told me she saw you at the station with a suitcase.'

'Alright then,' he says abruptly, flicking the ash onto a saucer. 'I've been to Milan.'

'What for? You've told me how dangerous Milan is.'

'I bought some sugar for the café.'

'On the black market, I suppose. What a risk to take.' She raises her voice. 'Look, I know you don't want me to work at the café any more, but that doesn't mean you cut me out of your life as soon as you step outside our front door.'

'It's not that I don't want you to work in the café, it's that it's not the Italian way. Mothers stay at home with their children.' He reaches over the back of the chair to get the grappa bottle.

She looks at him with sad eyes. 'Can't you see I need to breathe? Surely, just a few evenings a week wouldn't hurt, I miss it so much. Concetta Galli would love to earn a few lira looking after the boys.'

'Do you think money grows on trees?' he replies, exasperated. 'I have to take risks for supplies to make sure people keep coming into the café for more than just a cup of coffee, not to pay Concetta Galli for looking after the children in the evenings.'

Vivian takes one of his cigarettes, flicking the end of it nervously. Leaning her elbow on the table she lights up, slowly inhaling until it rasps the back of her throat. She releases the smoke out of the corner of her mouth. 'What am I to do?'

'Do you know that Eleanora Picatti is the head of the local Fascio Femminile?'

'No, what's that?'

'It's a separate fascist organisation especially for women. It is a continuation of the Piccole Italiane and the Giovana. A sort of doll drill for grown-ups.'

'Surely you're not suggesting I join.'

He takes a swig of grappa. 'Of course not! I mean that Eleanora will be watching you like a hawk because you're British, so the less you draw attention to yourself, the better.'

In a sharp and sudden movement, she squashes the cigarette into the saucer. Her eyes narrow to slits, and her cheeks flush. 'So it's one law for you and another for me. You won't sign the Fascio book, you can stand out because you're a man, you can take chances down in Milan. But not me. I have to do as I am told.' He bends down to unlace his shoes. In desperation she snatches up the half-full grappa glass and downs it in one gulp. He sits up in astonishment, and her eyes challenge his. 'I know it's assumed that my whole life will be sacrificed to you, any qualities I may have will be of little value, but I'm not asking for that much. Just a life outside these four walls.' He looks away. She stands up, her face twisted in disgust. 'I had thought you were different, but you're just like all the others.'

★ ★ ★

Giulio closes the window, places the radio on a small table against an inner wall and sits down beside Carlo and Luigi. He begins fiddling with the knobs. Vivian puts the stale remains of the Buccallato cake on a plate and brings it in from the kitchen, noticing while she does that the golden egg and sugar outside is no longer shiny. At least a few raisins are still lurking in the doughy ring. There has been an announcement that there will be a speech today, the 10th June 1940. The rumour mill will be stilled, the 'war question' finally answered. The tension in the room is palpable as they wait for the broadcast until at last there is a buzz, some whistling, and then the unmistakeable voice of Mussolini, hoarse and staccato, exploding into the room. 'Soldiers, sailors and aviators! Blackshirts of the Revolution and of the Fascist legions! Men and women of Italy, of the Empire, and of the Kingdom of Albania! Pay heed! An hour appointed by destiny has struck in the heavens of our Fatherland.' The crowd begin cheering.

'Poor sods, rounded up and driven into the square like animals,' says Giulio.

'Who's rounding them up?' asks Vivian.

Carlo turns towards her. 'The roads are cleared of traffic and Fascist party diehards go into offices and streets to drive the people into Piazza Venezia. They have to go or they're beaten.'

Vivian dips the hard cake in her cup of acorn coffee and listens. 'The declaration of war has already been delivered to the ambassadors of Great Britain and France.' She freezes as the baying crowd cry 'WAR! WAR!' The grand orator urges them on. 'We go to battle against those... who have hindered the advance, and have often endangered the very existence of the Italian people.' She stands and goes back into the kitchen, 'DUCE! DUCE! DUCE!' hammering at her brain, remembering how easy it is to lose one's senses amongst a crowd. She takes sips of water as Mussolini rides the moment. 'Italians! In a memorable meeting, which took place in Berlin, I said that according to the law of Fascist morality, when one has a friend, one marches with him to the end... this we have done with Germany, with its people, with its marvellous armed forces...' She returns to the others to hear the final act of political theatre. 'People of Italy! Rush to arms and show your tenacity, your courage and your valour!' Giulio snaps the radio off and bows his head in the silent room. Vivian looks across at him, her eyes seeking his but he keeps his head down until, at last he has to look up at her. She can see reflected in his eyes her own fear, the recognition that today will be as momentous for them as the day they first met, a turning point when everything would change. Although reluctant to cry in front of the men, she cannot hold back the tears.

★ ★ ★

The very next day it begins when the British bomb Turin, missing the Fiat factory but killing seventeen civilians and damaging the city. That same evening, standing in front of the wide-open window, Vivian feels the warm air caress her bare shoulders. The supernatural radiance of the moon reflecting on the lake seems ominous, the night eerily still, with just the undercurrent at the sucking water's edge breaking the silence. Now, when she lies down between the crisp white sheets, sleep won't come, and fear steals about her heart: she has become the enemy, and war does things to people's perceptions. How will Giulio cope? What will be done to them now that the bombs have started to fall? Throwing the sheet aside, she creeps through to the other bedroom and stays for a while looking down on the just-visible heads of her sons – what now for these angels? She kisses each one gently and then returns to bed, lying by the window with her hair gleaming in the moonlight.

As sleep finally flows over her, other images rise up too: emerging from white clouds of steam, a train like a large black monster is leaving Milan Centrale Station, and she, sitting on its front, is steering it towards a floral altar before which Father Colazzo is laying his hands on her bent head. A glistening jackboot dances to a violin as a marching band plays a soldiers' tune. Leonardo's face, full of fear, flashes by; and then a wine glass broken in eight pieces. The sound of fragmenting glass seeps gradually up through her dream and into her waking consciousness. She sits up with a start – glass is breaking somewhere, now, here in this room; there's a figure staggering across the room. She cries out. 'Who's there?' There is a belt being unbuckled, the swish of trousers slipping onto the stone floor and she can feel grappa breath hot on her face. She is about to scream when she recognises the smell of Giulio, grunting and swearing as his sweaty hands push her roughly back on the bed, his reason drenched in alcohol and overwhelmed by the aphrodisiac of danger. She succumbs to the inevitable, and her third child is conceived.

# Italy
## July 1940 to July 1943

'We have never been your foes till now. In the last war against the barbarous Huns we were your comrades... Many thousands of your people dwelt with ours in England; many of our people dwelt with you in Italy... And now we are at war. Italians, I will tell you the truth. It is all because of one man – one man and one man alone has ranged the Italian people in deadly struggle against the British Empire... That he is a great man I do not deny. But that after eighteen years of unbridled power he has led your country to the horrid verge of ruin – that can be denied by none. It is all one man... one man has arrayed the trustees and inheritors of ancient Rome upon the side of the ferocious pagan barbarians.'

*– Winston Churchill*
*Broadcast to the Italian People,*
*23rd December 1940*

Squinting down at the needle, Vivian finally manages to thread the eye and begins sewing buttons on Leonardo's shirt – it is all about making do now, patching and mending, and it will only get worse with another child on its way. She throws the shirt down and goes to the open window, looking out across the lake. It's darker than usual, although there are a few lights on (in contravention of the blackout regulations), and she can see the shine of car headlamps, out on forbidden journeys. A steady, distant rumble troubles the night air – the long, low growl of RAF aeroplanes flying over the Alps on one of their night bombing sorties over Milan and Turin – and she feels guilty, as though it is something to do with her personally.

A voice breaks the uneasy silence. It is Giulio shouting. 'Basta, basta va via.' The back door bangs and she turns around with a start to see him storm into the room, his face exploding with anger as he shouts. 'Bastards, bastards.'

'What's happened now?'

'Two cowards out there in big straw hats and black capes, with a paint pot.' He grabs her wrist and frogmarches her towards the door.

She pulls back. 'Don't do that, you're hurting me.' Outside, on the corner wall of their house, under the cover of the blackout, she can see someone has painted in large black letters: 'PERFIDIA ALBIONE.'

'Well, it's not my fault, Giulio, don't get angry with me. We can clean it off in the morning.'

'No. Now, while it's still wet.' In a commanding voice she has never heard before, he tells her: 'Go and get a brush and water.'

The atmosphere in Mandello is changing, she has realised that. It was little things, like Old Pepe the fishmonger slinking across the road when he sees her coming, and Mariella from the next street avoiding eye contact. But this feels different, more menacing: like being marked out as a plague house.

★ ★ ★

Vivian throws the last suitcase into the pony-trap – the luxury of a car being no longer available due to petrol rationing.

'Alright, boys, we're off,' she says, pulling herself up beside Giulio. Leaning back on the rough wooden seat, a wave of relief flows over her. At last they are getting out of the febrile atmosphere of Mandello, away from the melting summer heat of the lake and up to the cool of Resinelli. A wry smile crosses her lips as she remembers that exhilarating wedding-day drive in Alberto's red Alfa Romeo, the thrill of the moment and the future full of promise – oh, what a difference eight years can make. Still, how lovely it will be to see Francesca, who lives permanently up in the mountains in a small wooden house just to the right and down the hill from theirs. Sergio, her husband, spends a lot of time in Milan, so Francesca is pleased to have company. Vivian feels Francesca is the only true friend she has, and it is such a relief to have someone she can trust to talk to; added to which, Leonardo and Emilio are always happy in the fresh, sweet air of the mountains, running free with Francesca's two older boys.

Francesca has taught Vivian how to unpick old woollen blankets and make a skein, so they sit together under the shade of a chestnut tree knitting jumpers for the winter, when clothes rationing will hit them hardest.

Francesca turns her bright black eyes towards her. 'I've just remembered I've got some shorts for Leonardo – patches all in place.' As she jumps up and darts barefooted into the house, Vivian admires her lithe, sinewy body, the product of all-year-round mountain survival.

She returns with the shorts and a glass of lemonade. 'Here you are. Don't know whether they'll last long enough for Emilio, never mind the next bambino – when's it due?'

Vivian looks up at Francesca's thin, sharp face. 'I've got to get through the winter – March.'

With a weaselly glance Francesca asks. 'How is it with Giulio, now that he's sleeping with the enemy?'

Vivian strokes her stomach. 'I feel I'm losing my shape in more ways than one. I've just been absorbed into his life and then abandoned. He doesn't really talk to me anymore and seems to be out all the time.'

A fantail of lines form as Francesca screws up her eyes. 'There's gossip he's a sleeper.'

Vivian looks surprised and stops knitting. 'Has he got another woman? After all having a mistress seems to be an Italian custom.'

'No, not that. It means a dormant enemy of the regime.'

Vivian turns anxiously towards her. 'I suppose OVRA are waiting for him to wake up so they can get him.'

Francesca stops knitting too. 'Well he's got two black marks already – he's married to you and is the friend of a Jew.'

'And he won't sign the Fascio Book.'

'I know.'

'How do you know?'

'Word gets round,' Francesca replies in a knowing tone.

Vivian sips her lemonade thoughtfully. 'What could happen?'

'Arrest, a beating, a nice drink of iodine. If a man's got any secrets they usually get spilt.'

'You never know with him.' Vivian replies. 'He just might stick it out.'

'Well, in that case, if they really got nasty, he could get exiled to a village in the middle of nowhere, down in Puglia.'

They both stand up and walk over to the corner of the field, by the trees, where there are two old wooden beehives. Francesca bends down and pulls a glutinous shelf out of the hive. 'I remember him from school, always kept himself apart, full of opinions and as stubborn as a mule. He's clever, though, so I wouldn't worry too much about him. He knows how to look after himself.' She carefully pokes the honeycomb. 'He idolised his uncle Tomasso who died in 1918 fighting alongside the British in Trentino.'

Vivian turns towards her. 'Do you think that's why he came to London?'

Francesca extracts some honey from the hive. 'I expect so, and to see something different. Maybe it's why he fell in love with you.' She puts the honey, together with a bit of honey-comb onto a little dish and places it in Vivian's hands. 'Here, that's for the boys to fight over.'

★ ★ ★

That autumn, back in Mandello, Vivian parts and brushes Leonardo's fair hair over to the left of his blue eyes, noticing he looks pale and subdued. Seeing a bite mark on his left arm she asks him, 'How did that happen?'

'They did it – and they did this.' He points to the bruises down the back of his legs.

'Who is "they"?'

'Six of them on their way home from school – there were

some bigger boys too. In shorts, and pictures of Il Duce on their hats.'

'What did they say to you?'

'They shouted, "Piccolo Inglese, bastardo Inglese".'

Touching his arm, she lowers her voice, 'You point them out to me next time you see them and I'll sort them out,' but she cannot help seeing the alarm in his eyes at the very idea.

As Giulio finishes his plate of adulterated spaghetti, she decides the time has come and purses her lips into a point of determination. 'Have you noticed anything about Leonardo lately?'

'No, can't say I have.'

'Well you wouldn't, would you, you're out all the time.' She leans forward on her chair. 'He's being beaten up and called an "English bastard". He's being brave, not complaining. I think it's time for him to join the Figli della Lupa, like all the others.'

He gives her a dismissive look. 'Don't be ridiculous. Just look at that silly uniform.'

'But Giulio, when he goes to school he will have to join the Ballilla anyway,' she says softly. 'There's no escaping that.'

'Look, Vivian, you know very well it's all about indoctrination and the "great leader" Mussolini.'

'Maybe, but Ricca tells me when he goes to school next year he'll be taught the Fascist view of history, war is the way to live, no foreign words, that sort of thing. So he's going to get that, like it or not.'

'That's not the same as joining by choice,' he replies. 'You were never a conformist. What on earth has got into you?'

'That's not the point. It would show that despite having an

English mother, he is just another Italian boy.'

'No, never,' he shouts.

She stands up, suddenly finding herself shouting. 'You just don't get it, do you? Boys love camping, uniforms and singing. It's not a question of belief, it's simply safer to blend in with the group and join in the summer camps, the sports, the parades!'

Banging his fist on the table, he leaps up. 'I don't want my son being brutalised with the dregs,' and turns away from her. 'What are you thinking of, woman?'

She darts forward and plants herself right in front of him, hands on hips, eyes ablaze, voice on fire. 'I'm thinking of my child! It's all about you and how smart *you* are, isn't it – your obstinacy is making his life a misery!' She stabs her left forefinger towards him. 'Can't you see the children are outcasts because of you?'

Eyes red with anger, nostrils flaring, he seizes her left arm and pulls her in even closer to him, his hot breath on her skin, his twisted face in front of her nose. 'He is *my* son and you will do as I say.' He flings her hand aside, takes a step back, lowering his tone. 'What do you know? Your head's still full of that red book's nonsense – we're talking about the future of Italy here, not some fantasy.' She moves in and the crack echoes in his ears as he feels the sting of the slap on his left cheek.

He lunges forward and grabs her by the right wrist this time, looks blankly into her eyes and shakes her, whispering, 'You should have stayed at home.' When he lets go the skin of her wrist has turned purple and, having left the mark of his authority on her, he turns his back and leaves the room. She listens to his heavy footsteps on the stairs as he makes his way up to the top floor where he has taken to sleeping recently, leaving her alone while he goes about his work.

It is only then that she notices Leonardo has been sitting at the foot of the stairs, quietly listening to it all. He comes over to her and holds her hand, whispering 'Mama, don't cry.' She draws him close to kiss him.

★ ★ ★

Giulio lifts his dark glasses up so that he can fully appreciate the glowing hillside, full of burnished golden leaves shimmering in the breeze. As he walks on, out of the town up towards Resinelli, he thinks of how things have changed and of Vivian – those lovely eyes, the fun in London – remembering the bold, carefree woman he married. But nobody has a crystal ball, and who could have foreseen war with England? There's nothing that can be done to stop the boys being tormented. They're different because of her, and they'll have to toughen up. They are outcasts because of her, not me. He feels a little knot of anger forming in his stomach – why can't she see how Giovanni Farace would love to see them marching to his tune? His kind are ruining the dream she came to live. His mind goes over yesterday's conversation, the shouting and that slap, remembering how she had turned her head, but not in time to disguise the hurt that had been done with those few cruel words that he so regretted now, wounding words that from now on would lie and fester between them.

He looks towards the hillside, and sees the unmistakeable, formidable backside of Old Battista as the old man lowers himself down from the cart. The sun shines on the rusty metal pole and rotten fence as Battista secures the donkey's rope to the pole. Giulio approaches as Battista tightens the piece of string holding his greasy trousers up, wipes his nose on his sleeve and holds out a gnarled hand, covered in scratches. 'Ciao.' His face is so lined it looks like brown corduroy, his short, thick, white hair shines like wheat stubble in the glancing light. 'Where are you going?' Giulio asks.

'Lecco. Giovanni Farace wants his share.' He jerks his thumb towards two bags of wheat flour, six jars of olive oil, twenty kilos of tomatoes, thirty eggs, some sheep's milk cheese and a sack of apples.

'How does he get his share?'

In a gravelly voice Battista replies. 'At the ammassi. He unloads this lot and gives me a receipt for half,' He spits on the ground. 'Bastardo, he takes it to Mario's Trattoria so he and friends always eat good dinner for free – no ration cards. Plenty of steak and coffee for him.'

'You don't have to go, Battista.'

'I do, otherwise he'll chase me. He says to me my son will be taken to prison for selling stuff in Milan on the black market, beaten and made to drink castor oil and petrol. He does the same with others.' He holds his hand up, rubbing his forefingers and thumb together. 'He's a rich man.' Having pushed a sack into a safer position, Battista gives the donkey a nasty kick, climbs back up and, with a bitter smile, moves on.

★ ★ ★

Tossing the ration cards aside, Vivian sits on the sofa, kicks off her shoes and leans forward to rub the soles of her feet – how they ache after queuing for hours for a bit of grey pasta and rice and the 200 grams of bread allowed per person per day. She puts on a pair of old brown socks over her purple, frozen toes and covers her shoulders with a blanket to keep warm. There is still a bit of lignite burning in the stove but it will have to last, as there isn't much to be had. Concetta Galli has wrapped the boys up well and taken them for a walk and isn't back yet. Thank goodness twelve-month-old Federico is having a sleep; it hasn't been easy with him. He cried from the very beginning, couldn't settle and had trouble attaching to the nipple. How many nights had she spent, her breasts swollen with milk, walking him up and down the bedroom, holding him close and singing softly in his ear to ease his crying? How many times had she wished her mother was here to help, to take over in her stoical manner, to let her rest? It was no good expecting anything of Giulio. He loved his sons but this was women's work; he had to be up early to sort the café out and bring in the money, and so he remained sleeping at the top floor. Their intimacy foundered and when he did try to approach her she would push him away or turn her back on him, saying in an irritated voice, 'Not tonight, I'm too tired.' The last thing she needed was another pregnancy.

Sinking down on the sofa, she lies back on the pillows, shades of exhaustion visible beneath her eyes, contrasting with her sallow skin. To her surprise the door opens and Giulio walks in. Watching him throw his greasy jacket on a chair, a deep sadness wells up inside her. Who'd have thought that the handsome man in the double-breasted grey charcoal suit, with the flower in the buttonhole, would come to this? The sole of his right shoe is splitting away from its upper. Since petrol is scarce, and driving private cars is banned anyway, he has to walk or bike everywhere. The restriction of one pair of shoes a year per man is not enough. 'Any luck today?' she asks as he sits down.

'I've managed to track down some sugar. I heard old Agnes has more than she needs so I went over there and caught her at it.'

'At what?'

'Spreading the sugar out on the table and damping it down so it weighs more.'

'Did you tell her off?'

'No, she might not have sold me any.' He looks up from picking his dirty fingernails. 'Felt sorry for her, as the more she has, the better the chance of swapping for a bit of meat.'

'Only sugar then?'

'No, got some flour off Pietro – he's always got stuff.'

'Of course he's got stuff, Giulio – he's signed the Fascio Book. Why don't you listen to Alberto? You need flour and sugar for your work, not just for us, so why don't you just sign the bloody book, open a few doors?'

His voice turns flinty. 'How many times do I have to tell you? I'll never sign it. I'd rather buy on the black market. We'll manage with olive oil and wine from the Gallis, maybe a few eggs.'

'Jesus Christ, what will it take for you to see the light?'

'Let me spell it out for you. Giovanni Farace runs a little kingdom down in Lecco, speculating with people's lives, buying up goods just before they are rationed so that they disappear from the shops. Then he sells them for five times the normal price. There's plenty more like him.'

Vivian turns her face to the side in exasperation.

'How can I sign up for something like that?'

Vivian feels too weak to argue. 'All I know is that we have mouths to feed, and I'm the one who has to stand in queues for hours just to get the basics.'

Giulio stands up to leave. 'Anyway, you know how it is with Giovanni Farace and me – we hate each other.'

The door bursts open and in dash Leonardo and Emilio, running over to Giulio to clutch at his knees with delight. 'Have to rush.' Concetta says, as she turns at the door and smiles. 'Oh, by the way, Pa says to come over tomorrow. There's some space in the corner of the field for you to grow vegetables, raise some rabbits and keep a goat, perhaps?'

★ ★ ★

Feeling listless in the enervating heat of the July sun, Vivian pulls her sunhat down lower. Time hangs heavy on her and there is no let-up from the grind of domesticity. This isn't what she thought her future held. She can't see herself ending up like the other mothers, just wiping noses and bottoms, settling squabbles. It's not being balanced out by anything else. All the washing, feeding and ironing seems such a waste of time, she feels diminished by it and, like a dog on a leash, she can't wait until tomorrow: Resinelli at last. She turns to Leonardo and Emilio. 'Come on, time to go.' As if getting home earlier today would make tomorrow's departure come any faster.

Leonardo looks up, 'Oh please, Mama, a bit more.'

She puts her hand on her left hip. 'Just a few minutes, then.'

Federico rattles the metal frame of his pushchair, desperate to join in, as Emilio puts his thumb over the end of the drinking fountain and squirts water all over Leonardo's face. Vivian splashes some water over his bare legs and feet as Leonardo grabs Emilio and tosses him to the ground.

The next day, Federico stumbles through the grass towards Francesca, who sweeps him up in her small but muscular arms, repeating, 'Ciao, ciao bambino,' a few times. 'Ah, it is good to see you, come and sit down,' she says, putting Federico down. Vivian leans back against her favourite chestnut tree whilst Francesca goes across to her house. She feels safer up here, just listening to the sound of hens scratching at the hard earth and a lazy bee buzzing nearby; she expands her chest, deeply inhaling the mountain air and letting its restorative power fill her up. Now she can breathe freely, away from all those walls that have eyes, now no longer feel alone in a crowd. Francesca, fleet of foot and dextrous of hand, comes towards her with two shot glasses and some water on a tray, plus a clutter of knitting material and needles under one arm. 'Here, let's celebrate your arrival with a little Limoncello.'

Vivian takes the shot glass in her right hand. 'Cheers, then.' Francesca throws a pair of knitting needles down beside Vivian.

'How is it down in the metropolis of Mandello?'

'Not good. We've had a nasty poster stuck on our wall. There's a massive spider in the middle, its legs spread out in Union Jack colours, coming towards a mother as she cowers in a ruined city, defending her child with a rifle.'

'I've heard that was Giovanni Farace and friends.'

'How do you know?' Vivian asks, anxiously.

'Sergio keeps his ear to the ground in Lecco. Anyway, Farace's got a big mouth.'

'I'm afraid.'

'Don't be. Nobody really wants this war, you know.'

'How can you be so sure?'

'It's obvious things aren't going to plan. Mussolini flew to Libya to be ready for the victory in Africa, planning to ride into Cairo on an enormous white Arab stallion, but there was a stalemate. To pass the time he hunted sandgrouse in the desert with a machine gun.'

Vivian sniggers. 'How ridiculous.'

'He's becoming a laughing stock. He flew home looking old and grey. Some say he is ill with amoebic dysentary. Others say that he knows the writing is on the wall, is depressed and has left Rome with his little tart, Clara Petacci, resting in his favoured Adriatic resort, Riccione.'

Noticing Vivian is struggling with making a balaclava Francesca reaches over. 'You cast off here and then circulate.' She lowers her eyes first, and then eases them sideways towards Vivian. 'How's it with Giulio?'

'Difficult. With children and no money, the shine's come off the romance.' Vivian casts off. 'And you and Sergio?'

'He's never here. Always down in Lecco or meeting his friend Mario in Milan, so he says. Who knows. I'm used now and again, when it's urgent.'

'Has he got his own fancy woman down in Milan, then?'

'Maybe, or maybe not. I've not heard anything. Anyway,

he married me, took all of me, and now I do all the work up here.'

Vivian puts her knitting down and looks directly at Francesca. 'Is that what happens to women when they get married? They just get consumed like a plate of spaghetti.'

'Well, that's my experience.'

Vivian sucks on her teeth and looks thoughtful. 'I loved Giulio from the moment I saw him and then when I came here I fell in love with the beauty of the lake and mountains as well. It seemed like the promised land to me. But now it's all different. All the gaiety has gone, the Italians are miserable and I feel like a rat in a trap. I can't go to the café because of the children, because I'm British. I'm too tired to enjoy anything, and he has another life anyway with his work and whatever he gets up to in Lecco or Milan and it doesn't involve me. He has secrets he doesn't share.'

'Are you sure it's not another woman?' Francesca asks.

'I don't think so but you can never be sure, can you?'

★ ★ ★

The lake is just emerging out of the drifting mist as Giulio slips out of the back door. It's cold, so cold and this winter of 1942-3 has been particularly bitter – he can almost smell the desperation in the air. All the coal imported from Germany has gone to keep the factories going and the replacement, lignite, is getting scarcer. He piles up some logs outside the back door for Vivian and the boys before he leaves for work, relieved not to live in Milan or Turin where most of the cafés are closed. As he turns the key in the lock of Café Lario's double doors, some more flakes of green paint tumble onto the wet ground to be crushed under his boots. A third of the door is bare wood now and he can't find paint anywhere. Nothing is like it used to be – just surrogato coffee, a few pathetic looking cakes made of chestnut flour, a few bottles of beer and fewer of grappa, and that's it. The reception room is closed off; the dancing days are over. A cold sunshine whitens the dust on the counters as he and Carlo put the cups and glasses away.

'Well, how much did you get?' Giulio asks. Carlo kicks a small dark tan suitcase towards him, snaps the catches up and with a magnificent smile lifts the lid to reveal forty silver packets of Lavazza coffee.

Giulio snatches one up to his left nostril, sniffing langorously – 'Ah, the sweet smell of my memories.' He puts it back. 'How did you get it?'

Carlo places the flat of his forefinger to the side of his nose. 'My friend Mario's feelers get everywhere.'

Giulio smirks. 'What's it like down in Milan?'

'Miserable. They've made the parks into allotments. The big posters saying "EAT TO LIVE, DON'T LIVE TO EAT" have been torn down. People are sick of hearing about Mussolini's hangers-on feathering their nests while they are hungry and cold.'

'Like who?'

'Mussolini's mistress, Clara Petacci, is a Rasputin in skirts. She decides which government official is for promotion and who is for the chop. It's said her brother Marcello has made a fortune smuggling gold.' Carlo wipes a damp rag across the counter in front of him. 'Then there's the fact that Il Duce's son-in-law, Ciano, is one of the richest men in Italy. Everybody knows somebody whose son or husband has been sent as slave labour to Germany or to fight alongside Hitler in Russia while certain restaurants are still open – and full up with party officials and their toadies with their snouts in the trough.'

Giulio shuts the suitcase. 'And Mario? What about him?'

Carlo throws a copy of the Communist underground newspaper, *l'Unita*, down on the counter. 'He gave me this.'

Giuilio picks it up and flicks through. Its message is clear: now is the time to rise up. A National Action Front to fight Fascism has been formed, made up of a coalition of Communists, Christian Democrats, Socialists and other anti-fascists. This committee and that committee are forming and strikes are planned here and there. He looks up at Carlo. 'Is he a communist?'

'No. But he's a union member in a clothing factory. He says there'll be a big strike in Fiat Mirafiori in Turin soon, and he and others in Milan will follow suit. You see, the magic of Il Duce has worn thin – it's obvious he's losing wars all over the place. He's out of touch and people are plotting to get rid of him. There's even a joke doing the rounds about a small minnow being the last Fascist left in Italy. It was caught one day in the River Tiber in Rome but the fisherman, lamenting that he lacked olive oil, butter and flour for cooking his catch, threw the minnow back whereupon it swam to the surface, raised a fin in the Roman salute and cried gratefully, "Viva il Duce".'

Giulio pushes the suitcase under the counter. 'Very funny.' He tosses the newspaper on top and turns to Carlo. 'You must introduce me to this Mario.'

As the day goes on, the café gradually fills up with men, domestic refugees fleeing their despairing womenfolk who are trying to drum up the next meal while entertaining fractious children, trapped in chilly homes. Giulio looks across at a small group huddling around the hanging braziers, steam rising from their damp clothes, the perfumed smoke of the cherry, apricot and vine battling with haze of tobacco and stink of mouldy woollen cloth.

'What's news then?' he asks nobody in particular.

Fabio Silvestri shouts across. 'Last night the Soviets said the German 6th army have been defeated at Stalingrad.' He draws a finger across his throat. 'Crushed, kaput.'

Out of the corner of his eye Giulio notices Luca Bonetti, an old friend of Giovanni Farace, ease his way through the door like a mole hidden just beneath the earth's crust, penetrating quietly. His suit is shiny, his hair as glossy as a starling, and a neat little moustache lines his upper lip. Believing him to be a police informer, Giulio quickly changes the subject to football. 'What about the new man down at AC Milan? It'll be a disaster, won't it?' Since every man has an opinion on football, they all begin talking at once, except Luca, who takes his beer over to a corner seat and opens his copy of the Mussolini-owned *Il Popolo d'Italia*. As it comes up to 1pm, Giulio decides to play safe and abide by Il Duce's order that all cafés, bars and theatres should tune in to the radio at 1pm and 6pm to listen to official news bulletins. Yet there's no mention of Stalingrad, and everybody ignores the ruling to stop eating, drinking or talking, and to stand for the Fascist anthem, 'Giovenezza', which closes the broadcast. Nobody has been listening, and nobody even notices when the broadcast has ended.

Luca drains his glass and comes over, skimming the newspaper over the counter towards Giulio and stabbing his finger at the headlines. 'Pleased, are you?'

Giulio looks at the large picture of a bomb-ravaged street in Milan, full of dusty people dejectedly sifting through rubble. He reads how the Allied bombers have strafed people as they cycled home from work, showing no mercy, and then looks into Luca's night-black eyes. 'Of course not.'

As he leaves, Luca hisses, 'We know where your heart lies.'

★ ★ ★

Up in Resinelli, on Sunday 25th July 1943, Giulio sets off hunting, alone except for his brown and white gun-dog Nero, who runs on ahead fanning his tail excitedly. He is pleased to be let out of his compound. Giulio is almost as lean and hungry as Nero. With meat rationed to only once a week, hunting skills are ever-more crucial; there's never enough for three growing boys, Vivian and Papa. It quickly gets hot, so he puts his shirt in his knapsack, exposing the short-handled axe dangling from a worn brown leather belt holding his rough shorts up. He grips the shotgun in his left hand as he stalks across the meadows towards the woods, mulling over the situation. It's bad, really bad. First the embarrassment of the failed invasion of Greece, then the loss of the Italian Empire in Africa, and now the Allied Eighth Army has landed in Sicily – despite Mussolini's assurances that such a thing was impossible. Rumour has it that entire divisions of Italian soldiers are surrendering without firing a shot. He follows the dog's twitching bottom into the shade of the woods as Nero dodges here and there, snuffling down rabbit holes. Meanwhile, the constant bombing of Turin, Milan and even Rome means growing resentment against the Allies and, of course, against Vivian. All at once there is a blur of fur, the flash of a terrified eye; he aims and fires quickly. Nero scoops the rabbit up into his slavering jaws and runs to Giulio with rapture, watching, increasingly pleading, as Giulio puts the rabbit into an old piece of sacking and ties it to his knapsack. On they go, deeper into the cool of the hillside. Giulio is aware of the adrenaline subsiding and the familiar feeling of helplessness taking its place. There's no obvious way for Italy to turn. Not to Communism, which is the best organised of the political subgroups but demands a Russian-style revolution; not to the Liberal party, which is small and weak, while the Catholics want to return to a pre-Fascist world, and the King and the Army seem unable to act. He never thought it could get this bad. He stops at the edge of a clearing to reload the shotgun, lights up and takes a long drag on his cigarette. Nero squats beside him sniffing the air and then bolts to the right at speed, flushing out another rabbit. Giulio grabs the gun and leaps up, fires and misses, then sharply fires again and the rabbit flops down. Nero gathers it up and lays it at Giulio's feet with begging eyes, whimpering with anticipation as Giulio removes the axe from his belt and with one sharp blow severs the rabbit's head. Blood spurts onto his boots as Nero snatches the head, moves to one side and begins ravenously tearing it apart.

That evening all the doors and windows of Café Resinelli are open, people are lounging around the outside tables nursing their beer glasses as Radio Rome plays a medley of Italian romantic tunes – American and English music has been banned. A woman's warm voice, accompanied by a stringed instrument, floats on the sultry air. Giulio puts a bottle of grappa and four glasses down in front of the men playing backgammon on the battered wooden corner table. As he is gathering up empty cigarette packets from the floor the woman's voice stops abruptly, interrupted by a raucous: 'ATTENTION, ATTENTION.' A man next to the radio turns the volume up loud and Giulio listens in amazement as the broadcaster announces that at 6pm, on the orders of the King, Mussolini has been arrested and that Marshal Badoglio has been asked to form a new government.

The Italian National Anthem, not the usual 'Giovenezza', permeates the stunned silence.

The four backgammon men begin cheering, stamping their feet, smashing glasses on the floor and shouting. 'Down with the Duce! Death to the Duce!' Shots crack against the moonless sky as people run around spreading the news: 'Il Duce has fallen, Il Duce has fallen.' Words swirl in the hot night air. 'Where's Mussolini gone, what now?' Theories blossom. 'We've surrendered; the Allies are knocking at the door; Sicily is already theirs; the Germans have taken Rome; Il Duce is dead.' People form little worried clusters, some still in their nightclothes, and known supporters of the regime slink away, shapes melting into the darkness. Giulio watches the livid faces of a small group of bare-chested men singing as they gather round a flaming black Fascist flag burning on the grass:

| | |
|---|---|
| *Avanti a popolo, alla riscossa,* | Forward people, to the revolt, |
| *Bandiera rossa, bandiera rossa,* | The red flag, the red flag, |
| *Avanti o popolo, alla riscossa,* | Forward people, to the revolt, |
| *Bandiera rossa trionfera.* | The red flag will triumph. |

Having shut the windows of the café and locked the door – cleaning will have to wait – Giulio hurries away down the path towards Alberto's little house where he finds Vivian standing in her nightdress, her arm around Leonardo. He throws a half-burnt Italian flag over a chair. With a look of desperation he turns to her, pointing at the flag. 'See, this is what has become of Italy now.'

The pupils of her eyes are dilated and her voice trembly. 'Francesca's just left, and I'm afraid, Giulio.' She moves towards him, grasping his arm. 'Where are the Germans?'

'At the gates already, I expect,' he says, pulling his arm away. 'Who bloody knows.' He runs his fingers through his hair and flings the café keys onto the table. 'I'm going down to Mandello in the morning to see what's happening down there and check on Papa.'

Vivian moves closer. 'What, leaving us here?'

'Yes, you stay here, it'll be safer.'

'Can I come with you, Papa?' Leonardo asks.

Giulio looks across at his son, at the sun-bleached blonde hair flopping across large, clear, blue eyes, skinny summer-brown legs lost in patched and re-patched shorts – so obviously a foreigner, a walking target for abuse. His gaze moves down to the boy's feet, at the rough wooden soles held on with a leather strap – the zoccoli shoes of the poor – and his heart aches for his son. He puts his hand on Leonardo's shoulder. 'I'll sleep in with you and we'll go straight out after dawn.'

★ ★ ★

They find the shutters closed and Luigi up, sitting at the kitchen table. The day is already sweaty so his old vest looks damp, and the worn-at-the-knees trousers stained around the crotch. His face cracks in a smile and the thin, grey stubble sinks deeper into the hanging folds of his face. He stops sharpening an old knife on a stone.

Leonardo goes over to him. 'What are you doing, Nonno?'

'Just looking out for myself. I've been in all the time, there's been shooting all night. Look.' He hauls himself up, reaches under the table and picks up a large rock with 'traitor' written on it. 'This came through the window, so I shut the shutters and stayed in the dark.'

'Sensible,' Giulio says and looks across at Leonardo. 'Look after Nonno. I won't be long. I need to check the café.'

An air of euphoria still hangs over the town and groups of young males stride around with searing eyes, fingering triggers – after all, anyone could be the enemy. In the corner of Piazza Lorenzo, empty beer cans surround the remains of a bonfire on which a chair leg is still smouldering. His shoes crunch over discarded Fascist 'bedbug' emblems, torn from garments and crushed underfoot, and split icons litter the ground. The windows of the Mayor, Guido Morante, have been shattered and his desk torn apart. A punched-through portrait of Il Duce lies abandoned on the dusty ground.

With his heart in his mouth, he turns down the alley to Café Lario. God knows what damage has been done here. When he arrives, his eyes widen in surprise to see Carlo sitting at the front of the café, casually sipping from a Peroni bottle.

'I thought you might turn up after all the fun was over,' Carlo quips. 'Don't worry, no harm done.'

Guilio looks quizzical. 'How come?'

'I opened up last night, as soon as I heard the news. To-day's a national holiday, remember? Double celebration for us. I sold eighty per cent of the beer and we'll need to get our hands on more grappa.'

'Where's all the shooting coming from?' Giulio asks.

'There's a plot forming to march on the ammassi at Lecco – that'll be what it is.'

'Lock up the café and let's go,' Giulio replies.

A feverish group of men is gathering on the edge of town, and there is an air of menace; a gun could go off at any mo-ment. Giulio and Carlo join them as they move off. The crowd surges out of the town, Italians hungry to claim what is theirs. As they sweep down the hill into Lecco, now like an angry river of molten lava, three ammassi guards take fright and jump into a jeep, firing at them as they speed away. The crowd flows on until they reach the big metal double-doors of the store. As one they rush at them. The door rocks and the bolts rattle, but it remains firm. They pull back before surging forward again, and again, until the doors finally fracture and buckle, no longer able to hold out against this tidal wave of desperate determination. They stand on the threshold staring at the enormity of Giovanni Farace's agricultural kingdom – mountains of cheeses, sacks of rice and flour, jars and barrels of olive oil, eggs, salami, olives, wines, sugar, candles, coffee. Even cans of petrol. Then, it is every man for himself as they grab what they want most. Those who have had the forethought to bring a donkey are the winners, while others will have to limit themselves to what they can carry away. Carlo, who had the presence of mind to grab an old sack from the café, loads up with flour and rice, while Giulio chooses a can of petrol, a big bag of sugar and some coffee.

That night an interim government of military officers and Fascists impose strict martial law. There is a curfew and troops are told to shoot to kill if necessary.

★ ★ ★

'The House will have heard with satisfaction of the downfall of one of the principal criminals of this desolating war. The keystone of the Fascist arch has crumbled and... it does not seem unlikely that the entire Fascist edifice will fall to the ground in ruins... A decision by the Italian Government and people to continue under the German yoke will not affect seriously the general course of the war... The only consequence will be that in the next few months Italy will be seared and scarred and blackened from one end to the other.'

*– Winston Churchill,*
*House of Commons Speech, 27th July 1943*

Through the open window Vivian watches Emilio and Federico squealing with excitement as they play hide and seek with

Francesca's sons. The cicadas, lower down the hillside, grind and screech in the heat as she reaches out to a nearby tree and strokes a blushing apricot – the touch of Italy, soft and luscious, a touch of the exotic that she had longed for, that had once thrilled her. But not any more. She can't say that one day she was happy, then suddenly not, but rather that the steady encroachment of circumstance has worn away at her and Giulio, like water on a stone. She yearns for the good times, wants those old familiar habits to return – just a walk along the lakeside, holding hands; messing about on the water; baking in the café. She is lonely, and an unbearable sensation of the loss of him bears down on her. Their love has gone and their marriage has become empty. An artifice of mere survival in the maelstrom that is engulfing Italy.

Turning away from the apricot tree, Vivian goes inside the house, closing the door gently, and moves to an internal wall. Bending down, she slides her forefinger under the edge of the loose floorboard and lifts out the radio. Whilst more and more Italians switch on to hear the Voice of America or the BBC, Vivian never forgets that prison hangs over those who listen to a foreign radio station at home, and she is an obvious suspect. Sitting out of sight, she switches on. Placing her thumb and forefinger on the tuning button, she gently moves it to the right until somewhere, amongst the crackle of static, English songs can be heard. With meticulous care she manages to tune in and then leans her head on the back of a soft chair, seeking the consolation of memory. First of all there is a jokey war song called, 'I'm going to get Lit-up When the Lights go on in London', and then the smokey voice of Lena Horne singing 'Stormy Weather'. She closes her eyes, letting a wave of nostalgia sweep over her as snippets in the slipstream of consciousness come and go – the old kitchen table at home; the brown sails on the old Surrey Canal barge flap through her mind and she can almost smell the muddy river; that strange blue light in the Rosemary Branch bar flits across her eyelids, before metamorphosing into the reds and golds of the Ruskin window, and tears prick her eyelids as her mother appears before her, a letter in her hand. As the music dies away, she shudders in the silence as the dredged-up images fade to be replaced by Giulio's twisted face speaking with brutal truth. 'You should have stayed at home.'

She whispers to herself. 'What a fool I was, blinded by love.' She knows that all she can do now is to snatch at any snippet of happiness that may come her way, grab it with both hands, and enjoy the present, for who knows what horrors tomorrow may bring.

On Saturday Federico gives a shout of delight and runs towards Giulio and Leonardo, who are coming down the track leading a donkey with two saddlebags.

'What took you two so long?' Vivian asks, hugging Leonardo to her.

'Oh, it takes time to get stuff,' Giulio replies.

Leonardo rushes away to find Emilio and Stefano as she helps Giulio unload a small sack of rice, some flour, five eggs, two onions, three courgettes, milk, a flask of wine, acorn coffee, the usual low-fat rubbery cheese, six tomatoes, a small bag of polenta and four tins of missoltini – her favourite fish, dried with bay leaves. Finally, reaching into the bottom of the left pack she lifts out a real rarity. 'How did you manage to get the chocolate?'

'Had some extra olive oil and wine from the farmer next to Pa Galli in return for helping him dig a pit to hide some of the produce from Farace and his crew. I traded the oil and wine on the black market.' Giulio removes a small bag from the front of the donkey, opens it and offers it up to her. 'This beauty is for tonight.' She looks down into the dead eye of a fat, silver-scaled perch staring grim-lipped up at her. 'Miserable-looking sod,' she says. It feels good to laugh, for a change. He smiles, and glad to see a hint of the woman he once knew, he suggests, 'Let's have perch risotto – for old time's sake.' While Giulio takes all three excited boys out hunting for kindling, Vivian cleans out the fish and makes a stock from half an onion, olive oil, tomato, some sage leaves from the Mandello garden, and wine. The high-pitched squeals of thrilled children float in through the open door as the boys build a fire. She brings the fish and a small pot of olive oil out, handing it to Giulio. Federico is playing with a makeshift spinning top and Emilio is the one given the heady task of lighting the fire.

Leonardo stands back, maintaining a dignified expression of superiority as he watches Emilio's efforts. 'Papa, is it true Father Colazzo eats cats?' he asks.

Giulio chuckles. 'Who said that?'

'Oh, Stefano. He says all the cats have disappeared.'

'I don't think Father Colazzo eats cats, but I guess if you get hungry enough you might.'

The flames begin to dance, so Vivian goes back inside to sauté the other half of the onion in oil, stir in the rice until it is translucent and then pour in the fish stock. 'Ready' Giulio shouts, as he turns the perch over. She tosses the sage leaves on top of the rice and rushes out, keeping it hot, and it almost seems like old times again, like a family once more. For the boys there is even a little piece of chocolate each before bed.

After Giulio has gone to check on the café Vivian has a small bath and changes into a sleeveless blue cotton dress. Sitting outside on the step, her mind blank, just living for the right now, she enjoys that sensous feeling of warm night air against the skin, the wine flask beside her. She eases one of Giulio's cigarettes from a torn open packet, watching the paper flame urgently as she lights up. The tobacco makes her feel light-headed, as she tops her glass up again. When she feels ready, she stands up to take a walk in the moonlight, floating up through the wood, towards the café. She concentrates on the crunch of her boots as she gets closer, then catches sight of Giulio's face flitting in and out of the shadow of trees, and with a surge of desire runs towards him. He comes up close and she is lost in the exciting smell of him. He kisses her neck and breasts, pushes her up against the bark of a tree, lifts her dress and begins pressing his mouth savagely against hers. She bites his lip, amazed at how much she wants this, then puts her legs up round him and embraces him with a ferocity she has never known before, as they cling together in desperate pleasure, trying to recapture the past.

Throughout August Giulio leaves Fabio in charge of the café in Resinelli on the weekdays, whilst he and and Leonardo go up and down to Mandello, returning each weekend to continue the charade of a normal family life, seeking out the occasional moment of comfort with Vivian. Up in the fine mountain air, Vivian sits under a tree with Francesca, knitting, drinking lemonade and waiting for the potential terror of another pregnancy to pass. Francesca keeps herself well-informed and Vivian learns that despite the declaration of martial law, the Fascist office building in Milan has been ransacked; that crowds of people faced up to tanks and soldiers with fixed bayonets; that busts of Mussolini lay shattered in the road. In Turin, citizens drove a truck through the gates of a prison and freed both political and criminal prisoners. People come and go, circulating wild rumours; that Mussolini has got syphilis because of all his mistresses; that he is in fact dead and Hitler has committed suicide; that Rome is under German control; that Marshall Badoglio has surrendered, even though he said the war continues. They are surrounded by a sea of uncertainty. Nobody seems to know what is going on.

Finally, the last day of August arrives. Vivian leans against the side of Alberto's house with the sadness that marks the end of summer in her heart, brooding. Her violet eyes are fixed on the vermilion spectacle of sunset running along the sharp edges of the Grigna mountains. Usually a thing of beauty to her, today those edges have taken on a different hue; they have an ominous look of the bloody, serrated edge of a butcher's knife. She stays still, watching the crepuscular light of evening begin its purple descent of the mountain until, full of foreboding, she turns away and goes inside.

Next day, the barrocino cart is fully loaded. Giulio has hitched up the horse, and it is time to go down to Mandello. Vivian lifts Federico up whilst the other two boys climb in the other side. As the cart lurches forward, she puts her arm around Leonardo, drawing him close to her, knowing that bullies await him at school. Following the fall of Mussolini and during her mountain interlude, the Allies have taken the opportunity to increase their aerial bombardments of Turin and Milan and the full enormity of her dangerous position is now clear to her. She realises that the picture she once made of the dashing, attention-grabbing Inglese is not only a thing of the past, but from now on will also attract unwanted attention. To many Italians, she and her children will be the visible faces of the foreigner bringing devastation to Italy. While to both the Germans and Fascists, she will be the enemy within.

# Italy
## September 1943 to July 1946

'The Italian government, recognising the impossibility of continuing the unequal struggle against an overwhelming force, in order to avoid further and graver disasters to the Nation, sought an armistice from General Eisenhower, commander-in-chief of the Anglo-American forces. The request was granted. Consequently, all acts of hostility against the Anglo-American force by Italian forces must cease everywhere. But they may react to eventual attacks from any other source.'

*– Proclamation by Marshal Pietro Badoglio,*
*EIAR Italian Radio Broadcast,*
*8ᵗʰ September 1943*

It is now three days since the armistice and Vivian has been watching thousands of German troops passing down the lakeshore road, pouring through the Brenner Pass on their way to Lecco, Como and Milan, to supplement those troops already in Florence and Rome. Some have deflected into Mandello and set up a barracks in Molina. Out for a late afternoon walk with Federico, she sits down on an old stone seat at the side of the road as Federico picks daisies, giving them to her one by one for her to make a daisy chain, when she hears the dull thump of heavy boots. She turns her head to the right and there they are coming down the road, four abreast, self-assured conquerors in pristine uniforms, strolling easily through the town.

'Is the train for Milan late?'

The man turns his pointy face, framed by a neatly trimmed beard, towards him, letting his small, sharp eyes drive into Giulio's face like nails. 'It's on time.'

'Good, I'm meeting my friend Tigre from it,' Giulio says, before shouting across to the barman, 'Due grappa.' Tigre carefully puts the newspaper down on the counter before taking a packet of cigarettes out of his inside jacket pocket, revealing a Beretta handgun in the process, and offers Giulio one. He notices Tigre's fine, delicate fingers are smoke-yellowed and his hands are shaking slightly as he lights their cigarettes. They drink in silence until the train pulls in. 'Ciao,' Tigre says, mingling with the disembarking passengers as Giulio picks up the newspaper from the counter.

Giulio moves onto the platform and leans against the wall, his hand in his coat pocket, easing an envelope from between the folds of the newspaper. He notices James, in a workman's corduroy trousers and a cloth cap, pulled well down over those giveaway eyes. Standing further along, he can see Billy similarly dressed, a couple of people behind him. Giulio pushes into the train behind an old woman with a chicken tied in a basket, and stands in the corridor in case they need to make a quick getaway. He watches James and Billy squeeze their way past a crate of courgettes to stand next to him and surreptitiously slides the envelope (containing train tickets and false identification documents) into James's pocket. Giulio then gazes out of the window, watching night creep down the hills and cover the waters of the lake as the train pushes on through pillared tunnels, disappearing in and out of the mountains periodically. The tense stop at each station seems to last an age as people unload themselves and their baggage, but they are lucky tonight – no militia get on the train.

Finally the sign for Dervio appears, and Giulio leads James and Billy to the right out of the station, across the railway tracks and down to the lake. They cross to the corner of Piazza le XI Febbrano, by the side of the yellow church, before slipping down Via Bergmini where their boots clatter on the cobbles despite their efforts to be silent. Almost immediately, at the bottom of the alley, which faces onto the open lake, they run onto a shingly beach where a boat is moored. Giulio's boots sink into the flotsam and jetsam blown up against the shore as he whispers, 'We're going across to Rezzonico.' Slipping and sliding on slimy pieces of wood and rank vegetation, Giulio pushes the boat into the water, stirring up a rotting, reedy odour that oozes through the dank air straight into the lungs. 'A guide will meet us and drive you up to Carcente, where you will stay the night before your morning trek up the Val Cavargna. He will give you winter boots, socks, gloves and food provided by CLN. You will cross the frontier at Bogno – about twelve hours. You go down the Val Colla on the Swiss side to Lugano.' He untethers the boat and flings the freezing, slippery rope to James before adding, '500 lire for the guide, and for his Guardia di Finanzia friend at the crossing, the same.'

James holds the rope as Billy jumps in, then he pushes off hard, chucks the rope ahead, grabs the slimy stern and heaves himself into the boat. Giulio hunches over the oars, pulling away vigorously, making clean rhythmic cuts with the blades. They must clear the promontory to the right as quickly as possible and get out past the blue and white depth marker, standing like a barber's pole at the small harbour entrance. Fingers of mist cover the shoreline, so while he cannot see anybody, he can hear voices getting nearer. A shot pierces the silence, and fear arcs through his stomach as a bullet scuds over the water, spitting up spray before mass overcomes velocity and it sinks. Men shout 'COMMUNISTI FECCIA! TRADI-TORE! TRADITORE!' They are reloading and firing like machines, again and again. Another shot whistles past as James and Billy duck down.

'Keep hold of the rudder,' Giulio hisses as another bullet ricochets off the side of the boat, splintering the wood. He pulls harder on the oars as boots crunch on shingle, cries of 'BASTARDO! BASTARDO!' mingle with the click of re-loading cartridges and more shots. Whiffs of cordite mingle with the mist. 'FUCK! FUCK!' Giulio shouts as a bullet tears through the left arm of his coat before skittering off. He slash-es the oars at speed into the water, swinging the boat to his right so as to take advantage of a small breeze that will take them out of range into the middle of the lake, away from the hail of bullets.

And then they are gliding silently through calm waters, the current taking them down the western shoreline, past rocky outcrops and dark clumps of trees drooping into the waters edge. They drift on through the swirling mist, lost souls be-ing ferried to the isle of the dead, until cypress trees loom up through the night, and Giulio guides the boat through a vine-encrusted entrance to a jetty.

A man in a balaclava made out of hammered leather comes forward and points towards a black Fiat Topolina, scarcely visible up against the shrubbery,

'Buona sera Inglesi – avanti, avanti.'

At the top of the steps, James turns to Giulio and asks, 'What about you and your arm?'

'Oh, it's nothing serious, but I'd better fetch the boat another time. There is a safe house near, I'll stay there and go back on the ferry tomorrow.'

With a look of gratitude, James embraces Giulio quickly. Billy nods a goodbye before they walk off to the car.

★ ★ ★

Vivian pulls the back door shut and hauls Federico up onto her right hip, calling out to Emilio. 'Come on, let's go and see Carlo and Ricca.' It's then she first notices Luca Bonetti coming towards her. She has an instinctive distrust of this man, so instead of replying when he sidles up to her with, 'Ciao, Vivian,' she simply acknowledges him with a dip of the head.

Undaunted, Luca continues walking alongside her, flicking his tongue around like a lizard. 'I'm looking for Giulio, is he around?'

'No, he's gone to Café Resinelli for a few days.'

Luca turns his black pin-like eyes towards her. 'How strange, someone told me he was seen taking a train north a couple of days ago.'

Vivian meets his penetrating gaze. 'Well, they must be mistaken, mustn't they.'

'There's been a shooting up the lake. Are you sure?'

Her stomach turns over but she doesn't flinch. 'I'm sure,' and grabbing hold of Emilio's hand, she moves onwards, a mixture of anger and panic rising within – what would she do if Giulio has been killed? How would she and the boys survive? Luca drops away.

As she passes the requisitioned Villa Setmani, she notices the iron-spear-topped gates are no longer chained shut, the blue shutters on the three storied building are thrown back and the windows are wide open. Guns are propped against the palm trees and trucks have crushed the roses; malice pervades the air. Four German soldiers in SS uniforms are sitting under a huge magnolia tree, jackets loose at the throat, drinking schnapps and flicking cigarette butts into the scarred oleanders. She drags on up the hill, relieved to see Ricca, who is searching about the garden for eggs whilst Giuseppe works on his ever-expanding vegetable plot.

Ricca, noticing the exhaustion written on Vivian's face, greets her with, 'Ciao, let me take the bambino,' leaning forward to relieve her of Federico, stroking his glossy curls and kissing the rolls of fat in his neck so that he doubles up with a throaty giggle. Emilio runs over to dig around with Giuseppe as Ricca guides her to a chair under a tree and, after finding a ball for Federico, turns towards Vivian. 'What's the matter? You don't look well.'

'It's Giulio,' she blurts out, 'he's been gone for two days. He brought two British soldiers home in the dead of night and left with them the next morning, early, and I haven't seen him since.' Carlo is there, leaning against a doorway, listening, as she continues, 'And I've just heard there's been a shooting up the lake. I'm worried.'

Ricca looks back at her son. 'Come on, you must know something.'

Carlo has prepared himself for this moment. He puts his

book down and sits on the grass beside them. 'I've heard about the shooting. Rumour has it, someone was crossing to the west bank of the lake in a boat and shots were fired.'

In a firm voice Ricca asks, 'Is that "someone" likely to be Giulio?'

Carlo chooses his words carefully. 'I don't know. It's not safe to tell someone everything, as what you don't know, you can't tell.'

Vivian quickly intervenes. 'Yes, but is that the sort of thing he would be doing? What sort of boat was it? Was it day or night?' With a plaintive look, she moves towards him. 'Tell me, please?'

'I really don't know,' Carlo says, looking her straight in the eyes, 'But what I do know is that he has connections in Milan.'

Sensing Vivian's growing panic, Ricca says, 'Look, I'll look after the boys for a few hours while you go home. See if Giulio is back yet, and stay until Leonardo comes home from school. I'll bring them down later.'

The back door is ajar when Vivian gets home and as she tiptoes into the kitchen she sees a torn jacket on the floor, a blood-stained shirt on top of it and Giulio, with a taut expression on his face, bent over the stone sink.

'What are you doing?' she asks.

'Cleaning my arm, I've had a little accident.'

Relief that he is safe intermingling with sudden rage, she picks up a plate and hurls it at his hunched back. It hits the wall and slides down to smash on the floor as she shouts. 'How dare you lie to me!'

He turns his pinched face towards her. 'What do you

offers Alberto another grappa but his uncle declines, so he pours one for himself. 'You see I'm better informed than you think.'

Alberto takes the unique wooden box of the Toscano cigar out of his pocket, takes one out and rolls it between his fingers. 'So it would seem.'

'I also see you still have access to the nicer things in life,' Giulio says provocatively.

Alberto looks stonily across the room. 'Meaning?'

There's tension in the air as Vivian shakes her head slowly, widening her eyes in warning towards Giulio, but he presses on.

'Everybody knows you supply the Germans with the parts they need for their vehicles. You go in and out of Villa Setmani like a yo-yo.'

Alberto points his unlit cigar at Giulio. 'And everybody knows you go up and down to Milan like a yo-yo, getting your instructions.'

'That's not true,' Giulio replies angrily.

Alberto goes red, leaping to his feet and shoving the cigar into his pocket. He bangs his fist on the table, his large mouth wide open as he shouts, 'I *have* to trade with the Germans, otherwise they'll take over my business, and then it'd be forced labour. Curtains for me, and then what? Then where would you all be?'

Giulio leaps up. 'That's what you say – but that's not what it's really about, is it?' He bayonets his finger at Alberto's face. 'You're just an opportunist.'

'Please don't shout, you'll wake the children,' Vivian pleads, trying to push her thin frame between them, but too late. Alberto's large, muscular hand has already made a fist to grab Giulio by the shirt, pulling him across the table. He holds him there, eyeball to eyeball, saying in a measured tone. 'If it wasn't for Vivian and the boys, you'd be out of this house like a shot. It's only because I speak up for you that you haven't been arrested.' With a look of deep contempt he pushes Giulio backwards and a chair crashes over behind him. After picking up his things and heading for the door he turns towards Vivian. 'I'll do all I can to help protect you, but there's a limit to what I can do if he goes on like this, mouthing off all over the place.'

Vivian turns back to Giulio, still bristling, on the kitchen floor, and can't resist telling him he looks 'just like a turkey-cock, flexing its comb.' She picks up the glasses, 'Why do you always do it, always have to pick a fight with Alberto?'

Getting up, Giulio goes to open the window, letting some air in before turning round to face her. 'Because he's always on the make, that's why. Always doing deals. Offer him a thousand lire and he's anybody's.'

'That's rubbish, and you know it. Anyway, you're more than happy to borrow his cars and live in his houses, aren't you?' Vivian retorts.

'No choice.'

She slams the glasses back down onto the table. 'Can't you see he doesn't have a choice any more, either? The country is occupied, he has to do business with them or go under.' He ignores her. 'People depend on him for work, families and children need to survive. Why are you so wilfully blind?' She notices his right eyelid has begun to twitch.

'By God, I'm sick and tired of you all. Sick to death of

it. Family against family, all guns and leather boots strutting around. Look where it's brought you all, to the brink of ruin.' She turns away from him.

'Why the fuck don't you go home, then?' Giulio shouts at her retreating back.

Those words, like a stab to the heart, cause her to stop. Wheeling round she stands to face him. Her voice is quiet and icy now. 'Because I can't, there's no way out for me. I'm trapped behind the borders, trapped here with you.'

He comes towards her with a twisted grin, 'I love you when you are angry.'

She picks up a chair, her eyes like knives, and points it towards his chest, like a lion tamer in a circus. 'Don't you dare. Don't you ever touch me again.'

★ ★ ★

# Italy
## 1ˢᵗ December 1943

*In a radio broadcast to the Republic of Italy, Buffarini Guidi, Minister for Home Affairs, announces that all Italian and non-Italian Jews living in Italy are to be arrested, their property confiscated by the State, to be given to the poor; and Jews of mixed birth to be placed under special observation.*

The earth is loamy, rich and moist – the result of much care from Giuseppe Tandini. Giulio stands to the side as Carlo wipes the sweat from his hairline, tosses the shovel to his left, rests his right foot on the mound of soil and looks down into the small pit where the family valuables will be buried. Carlo lowers two tin boxes containing their three identity cards, some photographs, the family copy of the Tanakh, his own Bar Mitzvah yarmulka, most of their money, some gold, little bits of silver and all of Ricca's jewellery except her wedding ring, into the ground. Pushing the earth back in with his boot, he folds over some grass. As they both stand with heads bent like mourners at a funeral, Carlo tells Giulio, 'Remember this spot, in case I don't come back.'

Giulio feels a lump in his throat as he watches Carlo go to his father. He takes a last, long look at the late-autumn garden. It is a time of regret and sadness anyway, even without this additional loss hanging heavy in the air. Crimson leaves on the small vine rustle as Carlo pulls Giuseppe's sleeve and they turn away to shut the door on the setting sun.

Inside the house, Ricca is putting a few special photographs into a third suitcase which she ties round with a piece of string and then sets out on the table their last supper, remains of the garden produce: courgettes in a few dregs of olive oil, two tomatoes and scraps of the chicken strangled two days ago. Giuseppe breaks the stale bread and dips it in red wine. It has come to this, after all these years. Forced to creep out of their home like thieves in the night. The news that fifty-three Jews have been killed in cold blood at Meina on Lake Maggiore has made it plain it is time to go either into exile – to America or Switzerland – or to hide away. They can't just sit and wait in constant fear of a visit from the man from the Racial Committee.

The two suitcases are already loaded into Giulio's cart and darkness has arrived, so they must go. Giuseppe clutches the last bag, Ricca holds his other hand and, unable to look back, they leave the house. Carlo locks the front door, throws his own khaki knapsack on top of the other luggage, and they set out on their twilight journey out of the town as fugitives in their own land. Arriving at the Galli's, Pa Galli opens the front door and quickly ushers them inside as Ma Galli sets about getting an ersatz coffee ready for them, Giulio and Carlo bringing in the suitcases, hauling them up into the loft of the barn that stands at the side of the Galli house. As Giulio's eyes become accustomed to the dark, he sees that there is straw bedding covered with sheets and blankets on the floor, an old chest for storage doubling up as a table top, some candles, and a threadbare woollen rug. He notices a chamber pot in the corner and that the floor has been swept, but it smells musty, even so; like all dark places not made for human habitation. As Carlo puts a match to one of the candles, Giulio watches his pale face illuminated in the flickering light, his thin body taut and his mouth pinched. He turns away from his friend's sorrow and goes back down the ladder-steps.

It's time to go. Eyes glistening with tears, Ricca holds out her arms to Carlo. He hugs her tight. 'Don't worry about me, Mama, I'll be in touch through Giulio.' He squeezes Giuseppe's shoulders, unable to speak, and leaves. A small dust-cloud springs up as Giulio hits the donkey hard on its left flank and they move off in the silence of the night, Carlo's bitter face set like a stone.

★ ★ ★

Vivian is relieved to hear the back door open and looking at Carlo's dejected face instinctively asks, 'How are they?' He sits down in silence, letting the inadequacy of the words speak for themselves, as she awkwardly breaks a small polenta cake into pieces and hands him some. She tries again. 'What are you going to do now?'

He nibbles at the polenta. 'I have to get away before Giovanni Farace comes for me, rounds me up and takes me to Camp Fossoli.'

'What happens there?' Vivian asks, naïvely.

'It's a holding pen, from where people get shipped in cattle trucks to Germany.'

Giulio intervenes. 'He's coming with me up to Resinelli.'

Vivian raises her eyebrows sardonically. 'Oh, and Farace won't be looking there, will he?'

'It's a staging post, he's going on to join the partisans in the Grigna Mountains.'

Carlo's eyes brighten as he talks of action. 'They camp out

in caves. They're building up arms and ammunition to fight back.' A sad smile plays at the corner of his mouth. 'It's still early days, though.'

Vivian is afraid for this gentle soul, this intelligent man forced to abandon his dream of university and studying law. Now he faces a bitter winter in a cave, chased down by brute force and ignorance. She blinks tears from her eyes as she goes to bed.

Just before dawn, Carlo puts on a pair of woollen trousers, a thick shirt and a brown jacket. He repacks the spare pair of trousers, a woollen overcoat, two balaclavas, three pairs of thick socks, some scissors, a torch and a folding military knife. Slipping a bigger knife onto his belt, he buckles up and creeps downstairs so as not to wake the children.

Giulio is ready, with a hunting rifle slung across his shoulder and a knapsack on his back containing a small bag of food and some extra supplies for Carlo in it. He whispers to Vivian, 'Did you find them?' just as she emerges from the kitchen with a couple of packets of Populari cigarettes, and slips one into each of their knapsacks. She kisses Carlo quickly on the cheek and squeezes his arm before he and Giulio step out into the night and turn up away from the lake towards the mountains.

★ ★ ★

Giulio keeps his head down as the fog continues its imperceptible descent through the trees, smothering all sound and camouflaging the dawn, as they push on through muddy runnels and dripping branches, steadily climbing and skirting around houses so as not to be seen. Resinelli is deserted, and they slip in the back door unnoticed. The shutters remain shut as Giulio lights a candle and searches out the blankets – there can be no fire; the smoke would be visible. They remove their damp clothes and settle down to wait for the nocturnal knock on the door. Finally, it comes: a single tap followed by a triple one. Giulio leaps up immediately and his heart skips a beat as he opens the door to Marcello Maletti standing in the murky moonlight, wearing a pair of Russian galoshes, a waterproof military jacket and a fine Alpini winter fur hat that exaggerates his gaunt face. Seeing Marcello is alone, he relaxes his jaw and asks him in. Sitting round a table in conspiratorial candlelight, the bread and cheese looks so inviting that Marcello doesn't wait to be asked, reaching out his right hand.

Giuilio winces when he catches sight of the reptilian claw; forefinger and thumb closing round a chunk of hard bread, with three livid purple stumps resting on the table. 'God! How did that happen?'

Marcello glances up. 'It was thirty degrees below zero as the Russians chased us along the River Don. Il Duce didn't give us enough equipment.' He sneers. 'Boxes of fruit instead, marked "Apples from the Duce, sunshine from Italy". Our comrades, the Germans, laughed at us all the time. No gloves means frostbite, so my fingers went black and dropped off.'

As Marcello's large teeth tear at a lump of salami, Carlo asks tentatively 'And Roberto, what happened to your brother?'

Marcello swallows, his left hand fiddling with the blade of an army knife. 'Roberto had one shoe left by then, and the sole on the other one was flapping, our clothes were frozen stiff, we had no fat on our bodies and icicles on our beards. Just trudging through the endless snow in the retreat from Stalingrad. We were in a blizzard, and we saw a German truck coming towards us. We ran to it, trying to get in. But as Roberto grabbed the side, some German pig kicked his hand away.'

Giulio, noticing Marcello seemed to be choking on his words, opens his rucksack, removes a bottle of grappa and pours him a glass.

Marcello knocks it back and goes on. 'I still hear his screams, his leg was sliding along the icy side of the truck, tearing the frozen skin off. As his bare head hit the snow, he shouted "Go on, Marcello, go on," ' Giulio fills the glass again. 'So I went on, leaving him there with his blood congealing. Brown on the icy steppes.' He stares ahead fixedly for a moment and then looks up. 'I'll feel guilty forever.'

'But it wasn't your fault' says Carlo.

'Yes, but I left him there to die alone. I survived to escape at the German border.'

'There's no point in two people dying,' Giulio says, trying to comfort him.

Marcello bangs his fist down on the table. 'Now I'm a deserter, and I want vengeance.' His eyes are burning as he growls. 'I hate Mussolini with all my heart.'

In order to dispel the pall of impotent anger hanging in the air, Giulio crosses the room and picks up a map, spreading it out on the table. 'Show me where you are based.'

Marcello traces a scrambling path out of Resinelli with his claw, then follows it down into a deep gorge – a place of perpetual darkness in the bleak winter of these mountains, as Giulio knows – before climbing up again to a small ridge. 'We are here now – there are some caves which will be good for the winter, but in the spring we'll move around.' He looks up at Carlo. 'It'll be hard at first, but you'll get used to it.'

As they pack up, Carlo turns to Giulio and passes the dangling keys to him, 'Here are the keys to my home. Keep an eye on it for me.'

Giulio nods and puts them in his trouser pocket before bending and pulling up the hunting rifle by its strap. Unable to look directly at Carlo, he places the rifle in his hands. 'Take this, you'll need it.' He pushes the food parcel into Marcello's knapsack and as he watches them both melt away into the night he denies the tears forming in his eyes any release, letting the fury of injustice sweep though him like a flame instead.

★ ★ ★

The March wind is chill and the inside of the church is as inviting as a port in a storm. There are a couple of old women waiting to go to confession, fingering rosary beads, their devoted eyes turned in myopic adoration of the Virgin Mary. Giulio settles down a few pews from the back. All the most important staging posts of his life are reflected in these walls. Baptism, Holy Communion, Confirmation, Marriage – all overseen by Father Colazzo, who seems even more like a father to him, now his own father is in decline. He thinks back to the baptisms of his sons and the first happy party in June 1935. Mama was still here and Vivian so full of life, so different from the woman holding out that chair towards him, her eyes filled with despair and rage.

He pulls the purple curtain closed and enters the intimacy of the confessional box, a dark place where terrible truths are told, where secrets and lies are whispered. The Seal of the Confessional is sacrosanct, a fact even Il Duce acknowledged. After all, it was Pope Pius XI who said that Mussolini had 'given God back to Italy and Italy back to God'. Giulio kneels down, facing the grille. 'Bless me, Father, for I have sinned.'

Father Colazzo's ear and profile are just visible through the mesh. 'How are you, my son?'

'I've just come back from Milan, Father.'

'I hear it is full of anger and rebellion.'

'It's chaos. There is strike after strike. 300,000 workers in Turin walked out and the unrest has spread to Milan. There is graffiti everywhere and people marching around the streets, handing out leaflets and shouting "Peace, peace," and "No more war production for Germany." '

'Did you see Mario?'

'Yes, he's given me some new names. Do you know Marcello Maletti is back?'

'No. I'm surprised. What about Roberto?'

'He didn't make it – died in the Russian snow. Marcello has joined the partisans. Wants revenge for being sent into battle with guns that didn't fire and grenades that didn't explode.'

'Remember what the Bible says. "Avenge not yourselves, for vengeance is mine. I will repay." It is an unhealthy emotion. However, there are other reasons for joining the partisans. Such as freeing us from Nazi occupation.'

'Have you got anything for me to take up?'

'Some blankets, socks, cheese, matches and cigarettes. I'm hoping to get them a radio one day soon. Collect them from Dante's house. Now, how is it with you, my son?'

'Vivian is angry. She spits out words at me, firing up without reason. She won't let me near her.'

'Be patient with her. You must never force yourself on a woman. She'll come round in the end. Remember, women are emotional and they can't always see the bigger picture. That's why St. Paul said, "Wives must submit to their husband, as he does to the Lord."'

'She wants me to tell her everything I'm doing.'

Father Colazzo's voice is soothing. 'It is prudent not to share your plan of action with her; as, that way, she can't gossip. A woman is most fully a woman when she is a wife and mother, which is why her life should be kept to the domestic sphere. Of course, Italian women understand that better than the English.'

'Thank you Father. And I have one more thing before I go. Leonardo wants to know if you eat cats?'

Father Colazzo laughs throatily. 'Tell him there aren't any left to eat, so, no.' He then makes the sign of the cross. 'I absolve you from your sins, in the name of the Father, and of the Son, and of the Holy Spirit.'

★ ★ ★

'Assistance to the Italian partisans has paid a good dividend. The toll of bridges blown, locomotives derailed, odd Germans eliminated, small groups of transport destroyed or captured, small garrisons liquidated, factories demolished, mounts week by week, and the German nerves are so strained... that large bodies of German and Italian Republican troops are constantly

tied down in an effort to curtail Partisan activity. Occasionally pitched battles have been fought, with losses to
the enemy comparable with those they might suffer in a
full-scale Allied attack.'

*— Report from General Alexander's headquarters
(15th Army Group), May 1944*

Vivian looks across the kitchen table at two more strangers
eating in her house. Having finished the pasta pomodoro, the
thin teenager, Alexei, pushes a thin roll-up between his tufty
beard, puffing on it nervously before repeatedly flicking the
cigarette with his forefinger. Vivian watches the ash settling
around his feet like a dirty snowfall. He takes out a copy of
the latest *l'Unita* newspaper and studies it closely, seemingly
oblivious to her presence as she clears the plates away.

'Let me help you,' says the other man, the tall, elderly lawyer, putting his hands on the table as a prelude to standing up.

'No. Don't worry. I'll do it.' As she picks up the knives
and forks, Vivian feels his hooded hawk-like eyes on her, and
looks up to see that his huge nostrils are full of hair. There is a
proudness in the sharp line of his jaw. 'What brings you here?'
she asks.

'I made the mistake of letting the CLN use my office as a
safe house, but my neighbour turned out to be an informer. As
the Gestapo burst through my front door, I ran out the back,
and here I am.'

Giulio enters the room. 'It's time we were going,' and
then, like a military commander, 'Vivian, get the clothes out.'

With a great show of effort, she pulls the chest away from

the wall, takes out an armful of clothing and boots and throws them on the floor resentfully. Slowly sifting through, the lawyer gathers a selection up in his arms and moves into the hallway. Like a snake sloughing off its old skin, he removes his city suit, puts aside his pocket-watch and handkerchief, and folds the suit into a neat pile. He pulls on some loose-fitting brown woollen trousers and exchanges his useless, gleaming leather shoes for lace-up peasant boots. Having put on a hunter's jacket and slipped the new identity card into the pocket, he comes back into the kitchen to ask Vivian, 'Can I have a needle and thread?'

'Here you are,' she says, threading it for him, and then stands watching his graceful fingers sew several thousand lire into the lining of a small waistcoat. He opens a pale tan briefcase, removes a bundle of papers, some photographs, a small figurine and a silk handkerchief and then looks up at her.

'I don't suppose you have an old suitcase?'

'No, sorry, but I have something else that might do.' Vivian returns, holding open a frayed, dusty flour sack as he carefully places his precious objects inside. All he needs now, she thinks, is a few days' growth of stubble and he'll safely be able to join the ranks of Mussolini's mountain incognitos, dragging their pitiful mementos from pillar to post.

Alexei opens his stained canvas bag and throws a bunch of tatty pamphlets on the tabletop in front of Vivian. He looks sickly, his pasty skin tautly stretched over prominent cheekbones. He thrusts a pamphlet headed 'Communism Will Set You Free' into her hand. 'This is what it's all about.' She reads. 'Let the ruling classes tremble at a Communistic revolution. The proletarians have nothing to lose but their chains. They have a world to win.' Further down: 'Capitalism: Teach a man to fish, but the fish he catches aren't his. They belong to the person paying him to fish, and if he's lucky, he might be paid enough to buy a few fish himself.'

She looks into his flashing, fervent eyes. 'You really believe in this?'

'Yes, it's the truth.' He stoops over the pile of clothes, a few locks of curly black hair snaking onto his shoulders, as he selects an overcoat and a pair of steel-capped boots. He stuffs his pamphlets back into his canvas bag and stands, tense with anticipation. 'Ready.'

Vivian follows Giulio out into the hallway and hisses. 'Shouldn't you find out more about Alexei? He looks so vulnerable.'

'You don't think he would tell us anything, do you?'

'Maybe not but he seems strange – elsewhere. It can't be a good idea to send someone so young up into the mountains.'

'Better to be up there than wait to be press-ganged into Mussolini's new Republican Army.' He picks up his rucksack. 'Bring the food bags, we need to go.'

★ ★ ★

As she takes her place in the bread queue, Vivian's back aches and her legs feel like lead. She's already spent two hours waiting outside the Latteria to get some milk - there's never enough milk for the children, even though Luciano, the milkman, always sneaks a little extra in the enamel jug she holds out, always exceeding the ration amount for those with children. She watches the German guard ease his rifle into a more comfortable position on the shoulder, his bored blue eyes scanning up and down the bedraggled line of hungry people.

A commotion starts up behind her, and Vivian turns round to see a wrinkled woman with grey wispy hair eyeing her fiercely, pushing a newspaper towards her. On the front page she sees a picture of a small child covered in blood, holding a shredded doll. Scanning quickly, she reads that Allied planes have apparently been dropping toys, sweets and lipsticks packed with explosives so as to maim Italian women and children. Someone pushes Vivian from behind, another calls out 'Go home, bastard,' and as two other women begin to jostle her, a broad-shouldered middle-aged woman in a headscarf comes up close, sucks her sunken cheeks in even further, purses her lips and spits full in her face. Vivian instinctively recoils, but puts her hand up too late, and the warm gelatinous spittle slides down her left cheek before settling in a slimy pool on the shoulder of her brown woollen jacket. As the women begin to circle around her, jabbing at her with their fingers, she hears a gunshot and the staccato 'BASTA! BASTA!' of the German soldier. She feels his firm grip digging into her arm as he frogmarches her away to the front of the queue where she receives the outheld hard, black loaf of bread, her trembling hands fumbling it into her string bag. Like a furtive animal she slinks away as a woman steps forward, shouting, 'Foreign bitch!' and casts a stone at her ankles.

★ ★ ★

'Captured partisans are not prisoners of war, and will be shot on the spot. Civilians will also be shot who: supply partisans with i) food ii) shelter iii) military information (spying); carry arms (including hunting weapons), ammunition, explosives or any other war material, or who do not report to German Authorities weapons, ammunition, etc. concealed by others; commit hostile acts of any kind against German Armed Forces.'

*– Order of Field Marshal Albert Kesselring, July 1944*

The sonorous sound of the big Angelus bell booms out three times into the gathering evening mist as Vivian approaches San Lorenzo church. Her feet are already wet and every cobblestone seems to pierce the thin soles of her canvas shoes. The bell rings out another three times. Glancing towards the lake, it has already disappeared in the heavy, dripping autumnal evening, and the sorrowful sound of the final three tolls drags her spirits down even further as she opens the church door. An immediate wave of relief floods over her; in the protective embrace of its perfumed warmth, she feels like a baby returning to the womb.

She knocks gently at the inner door and waits, but starts when a bulky, slow-breathing figure emerges from the shadows at the side.

'Don't be afraid, my child,' comes the soothing voice of Father Colazzo.

'Sorry, Father, I'm always on edge these days,' she replies.

The scent of incense becomes overpowering as he comes closer and, in an intimate gesture, holds her chin, taking in her sallow skin and the dark rings under her eyes. 'You've grown thinner since I last saw you.'

She moves backwards. 'I'm not well, really, that's why I'm here. I need to talk to you.' He takes her hand and they move into the presbytery. The chair grinds against the stones as she pulls it out to sit opposite Father Colazzo, at an old square oak table covered with stains and cuts. They are surrounded by shadows and darkened corners; it's like sitting opposite half a person, as the left of the priest's face is in shade, the right side emerging only in parts from the blackness as shafts of light from a tiny, high-up window hit his temple, cheekbone and nose.

He picks up a glazed ceramic jug and pours a little golden wine, candlelight glinting off the glass as he holds it out to her. 'Here, some communion wine – unblessed, of course.'

Pulling herself out of her trance, she turns her eyes away from the flame of the candle to see Father Colazzo breaking a lump of dry bread in two. It is too hard to chew, but dipping her piece in the wine and sucking on it, like a child, until it dissolves in her mouth, allows her some time before the words come tumbling out. 'Father, I'm really worried about what is going to happen. You see, Giulio is in touch with people in Milan, and they are sending escaped prisoners up to him so that he can pass them onto others who will take them over the border to Switzerland. He doesn't tell me everything, but I know about Marcello Maletti and the others gathering in the mountains. I know it's dangerous for my family. You must have seen the posters plastered around the town, saying captured partisans will be shot, people who help them will be shot, relatives can be taken as hostages. I feel like an out-cast anyway. I've been spat at, the boys are being kicked and bullied, we can't go to the Galli's any more. Fascist spies are

get some sleep, and they turn in. The next day, as dawn is about to break, Giulio hands over the radio rucksack. 'So, what's the spring plan?'

'Sabotaging railway lines and bridges. We've already captured a truck full of boots. Worth their weight in gold, of course. The kid, Alexei, wants more drama, like a hit-and-run on barracks. We are trying to keep away from villages so that ordinary people don't suffer German revenge for supposedly supporting us. I've seen terrible things.'

'Such as?' Giulio asks.

'One man's naked body thrown on the roadside with his crushed testicles beside him. A priest with his teeth smashed in, a chestnut shed on fire with two men and a woman inside.' He looks down at his feet. 'Then there's the rapes.'

In the silence, Carlo hangs up the little sack of salami, cheese and wine that Giulio has brought up for him, onto the radio rucksack and then hands Giulio a letter. 'Here's another one for the confessional box,' and darts out of the door. With a lump in his throat, Giulio watches his thin frame, dodging and cutting through the budding woods, like a fox on the run, until he is out of sight.

★ ★ ★

'Where partisan bands operate in large numbers hostages are to be taken first from the population of the district in which they appear. In the case of brutal attacks these men will be shot. This fact will be made known to the population when hostages are arrested. Culprits or leaders will be hanged in public... If German soldiers fall victim to attack by civilians, up to 10 able-bodied Italians will be shot for each German killed.'

*— Order of Field Marshal Albert Kesselring, July 1944*

Rastrellamento songs echo through the thin air and the mountains are on fire as German units from Bergamo and Milan join their fellow travellers, the Italian Black Brigades, in torching mountain refuges, burning homes and massacring villagers. Vivian flares her nostrils at the sulphurous smell of cordite wafting through the labyrinthine ravines and caves as they flush the partisans out. Standing on a ridge high above the town, she sticks her hands in the pockets of her old light-pink cotton dress and turns towards the sun, a light mountain breeze brushing her auburn curls. Distance alters perspective, and as she looks down into the summer cauldron of the valley, the small towns dotted along the vertiginous sides of the lake seem like anthills waiting to be swept away in the surging wave of the advancing Allied army now making its way towards the River Po. To her the glittering surface of the lake now simply represents the anvil of sorrow that Italy has become, and she has long known there is no way out for her. Churches may toll their bells, but the ears of Generals planning Operation this or Operation that are deaf to them and, in the scale of things, she is insignificant, her fate of no consequence. Fear is a constant companion now and her throat tightens as she remembers the story of the savage murder of an Englishwoman for no reason other than being married to an Italian farmer in Quoto, Tuscany. Her face grim and her eyes downcast, she turns her back on the lake and goes in search of Francesca — today, they are going to knit a set of balaclavas for the local children to wear in winter.

Francesca is leaning back against the side of the house. 'Just cooling down a bit,' she says, removing her rough, tough feet from a bucket of cold water and wiggling her toes. She turns her head and shouts towards the open door. 'Come outside. Vivian's here.'

Sergio is a short, compact man who moves in a decided manner. Vivian judges him to be about ten years older than Francesca. He looks like someone who knows how to look after himself on a dark night in Milan. He sits down on the step next to her. A smile cracks his coarse face. 'How are you?' Vivian notices that his broad hand grips the German beer bottle firmly and that his knuckles are bruised.

'Hot.' She smiles. 'It's a surprise to see you.'

'I'm having a break from Milan – half the city's bombed out, full of shells.'

'Been in a fight?' Vivian asks, glancing down at his knuckles.

'It's tense down there. You only have to look at someone twice and they're up for a scrap.'

Francesca passes Vivian some wool and needles and nudges Sergio. 'Tell her about the Koch squad, then.'

'Pietro Koch is one of Mussolini's men, an Italian with a German father, hooked on cocaine, a drug dealing ex-soldier. When Rome fell to the Allies in June, he moved his squad out to Florence, and then Milan. He's got his own private prison and torture chamber.' Sergio wipes the sweat off his face with the back of his left hand. 'There's stories about matchsticks forced under toenails and then set alight, electric currents, prisoners in tiny cells with no lights, no water, nothing. If you survive, you get sent to Germany.'

Francesca interjects. 'Yes, but tell her what happened to you.'

'When I got to the factory doors there was a group of men chanting slogans. One stuffed a leaflet into my hand just as a van with six men pulled up. They charged at us with clubs and knives. Someone shouted, "It's the Koch squad – run!" Some big-boned, flat-faced man grabbed a half-broken brick from the rubble and threw it at at me – like that.' Sergio flings his beer can across the front of the step with force. 'He bawled insults as his dog bit my leg. I booted the dog away.' He stands up, kicking the side of the step hard. 'Like that, and as he bent down to pick up the brick again I punched him hard on the side of his head. The blood ran through his thick eyebrows into his eyes, so I had time to get away.'

Vivian can think of nothing to say, but luckily they are distracted at this point by Giulio, running across the field towards them, Nero with his tongue hanging out, barking as he chases his heels. Giulio's chest is heaving. 'Just heard on the radio.' He has to stop to catch his breath before speaking again. ' There's been an assassination attempt on Hitler in his Wolf's Lair. Bomb planted under a table at a meeting by some Colonel.'

'Any injuries?' Sergio asks.

'Minor burns and concussion.'

'Pity.'

'The German News Agency says he is fit enough to meet Benito Mussolini, who has just arrived, and that he must be under the protection of a divine power.'

Sergio roars with laughter. 'Thank goodness for that, then.' Putting his arm around Giulio's shoulders, he says, 'Come on, let's go and get a beer.'

'I'm glad someone thinks it's funny,' Francesca says, watching them go.

* * *

As Giulio makes his way along the lakeside, it seems just like any other autumn day – the bushes aflame with berries and an old woman in a ragged skirt gathering a few nettles to add to her risotto. He hears dogs barking as he turns left into a small piazza, suddenly finding himself amongst a small crowd, frozen under the gruesome spectacle of a tousle-headed young man swinging in a noose like a dead bird. The blackshirts have arrived in his own village, and set up a scene of execution. To the right of the newly-erected gallows there is another, darker man, his hands tied behind his back, screaming, 'I'm innocent, I'm innocent!' as an executioner thrusts his head through a noose. A large bull of a man stands with jackbooted legs akimbo, keeping a tight hold on the straining leash of two snarling German Shepherds, who occasionally lunge their ugly muzzles towards those nearest to them. The rope is slung over the gallows and two men pull it hard until the shoeless man, his head forced to one side by the thick cord, rises from the earth and the screaming stops as he loses consciousness.

Meanwhile, on the other side of the piazza, the passenger side of a small truck swings open and Captain Bartoli of the Brigate Pavoni jumps briskly down. He rubs two fingers along his mouth before passing them through his slick, black hair. The skull with a knife in its teeth, embroidered in silver thread on his blackshirt pocket, glows in the softening sunlight. He nods, the back of the canvas-covered truck bangs down, and Marcello Maletti is thrust out, his body bearing all the hallmarks of a brutal interrogation. There is murmuring amongst the sullen crowd as they recognise one of their own. Giulio's heart bangs against his ribcage as he watches Marcello stumble and fall on the ground, his battered and bruised face hitting the cobblestones. Giulio, aware that Luca Bonetti is staring at him, shows no emotion and resists the urge to run to Marcello, his heartbeat slowing as he catches sight of Father Colazzo's familiar biretta progressing through the crowd. The priest strides forward, a prayer book firmly grasped in his left hand, and kneels down to place his right hand gently on Marcello's head. He leans over him to make the sign of the cross and barely has enough time to administer the last rites before rough hands snatch Marcello away to force him down onto the waiting chair, facing backwards, his legs splayed apart, hands roped. The brass ammunition ribbons lie like devil's teeth across the blackshirted chests of the three-man firing squad as they line up and take aim. On signal they fire and Marcello's body starts upwards before slumping forward like a rag doll, his head propped up on the back of the chair. But he is still breathing so Captain Bartoli steps forward, the handgun sitting snugly in the palm of his hand. He slips the catch at the base of the stock and slides the magazine home, a repellant gleam in his eyes as he lifts the gun close to the right ear and administers the coup de grâce. He returns to his truck as a lackey places a placard marked DESERTER across Marcello's back and secures it by plunging a knife deep into the flesh.

Wheels screech and dust swirls as the death squad sweeps out of the piazza and the crowd begins to slowly disperse. Giulio leaves quickly, knowing only too well that Luca Bonetti will follow him. As he turns the corner he recognises Marcello's mother running towards the piazza and holds his breath, waiting for the scream of anguish.

★ ★ ★

Bending her head against the icy wind, Vivian hoists a whingeing Federico onto her right hip for the last leg of the walk home, dangling the small sack of flour in her other hand. It feels like a lump of lead today, and she speculates on what the additive could be this time – maybe marble dust. She locks the front door behind her, but just as she is about to put a saucepan of water on the stove, two sharp knocks on the back door make her start up. Who could it be? Nobody visits, these days, and she's alone with the child. Two more hard, masculine knocks are accompanied by a whispered, 'Open up.' Federico hides behind the edge of her skirt as she makes her way down the dingy corridor, feeling a vein in her forehead pulse as she leans her ear against the door and in a low voice asks, 'Who is it?'

'A friend. Quickly, open up.'

Summoning up all her courage, she grips the handle firmly, turns the key and the door bursts open, almost knocking her and Federico over. A man, his face covered by a black scarf so that only his coppery eyes and ragged eyebrows are visible, swings round to face her.

Her hands sweat. 'Who are you?'

His voice is sharp, like a blade. 'You don't need to know.'

She leans her back against the wall. 'Have you come to take me away?'

'No, I've come to give you this,' he says, handing her a piece of white card. 'Listen, there is a rastrellamento, starting tomorrow, in Como, Lecco and Mandello. I've seen the list – Giulio's on it.'

Her breathing steadies as they stand facing each other, the sense of danger floating in the air between them, until she looks down at the bulging eyes of her small child, and gently strokes his hair. 'So, at last, the reckoning arrives.'

'I must go,' the man says, opening the door and looking about him.

She only has time to say, 'Thank you,' to his retreating back before he disappears.

She lights the small oil lamp on the kitchen table, sits Federico on her knee where he quietly sucks his thumb, leaning his head against her breast, and reads the white card:

Giulio Ricci: son of Luigi Ricci.

Born Mandello-del-Lario 5 March 1908.

Height: 178cm. Eyes: dark, honey brown. No moustache or beard.

Occupation: pasticciere, family business.

Travelled to Paris and London 1931/2.

Married an Englishwoman 19th March 1933.

Known associate of Carlo Tandini, a Jew and suspected partisan.

Activites report: unknown people seen at his house, arriving at night.

Suspected links to CLN in Milan. Leaves Mandello for days at a time.

Part of network of safe houses for Communists, deserters and others. Aided POWs to move to Swiss border. Role of wife not known but likely to sympathise with Allied Forces and assist her husband in supply of food and clothing to resistance forces. Both suspected of listening to Radio Londra.

Realising the writing is definitely on the wall, waves of anger, despair and panic flood over her. She remains static, staring fixedly into the flame of the lamp, holding the sleeping child, until finally something of her old self returns within and her mood suddenly transforms as the immediacy of danger boosts her vitality. The desire for self-preservation and that of her family predominates. Urgency of action takes over. It is quite clear to her that the only place they can go to in a hurry is Resinelli. She lays Federico down on the bed and begins to pack – a suitcase for the children, and her little black leather one from England for her and Giulio. The food will have to go up in a sack. There's no petrol for cars, so it'll be up the mule track with a donkey – just like the Holy Family. A bitter little smile crosses her lips; no doubt Father Colazzo would approve of such a Biblical reference. She lays out clothes suitable for the children on a winter's trek. Two pairs of trousers each, two jumpers, gloves, two pairs of socks and an overcoat. She is so preoccupied that she doesn't hear Giulio, Leonardo and Emilio come in, and is surprised by Giulio's peremptory question.

'What on earth are you doing, woman?'

She looks up and says ironically, 'We are going for a little winter trip.'

Leonardo comes up to her excitedly. 'Oh, that's good news. Because school is shut, for at least a week.'

She smiles at him. 'Run along, would you, and set the table.' She pushes the door closed and faces Giulio. Her voice is calm and steady. 'It's time for you to face the music. You are on the rastrellamento list – it starts tomorrow.' She passes him the white card. 'Here, take a look at this.'

He snatches it and reads. 'How did you get hold of it?'

'A man came by. He's seen the rastrellamento targets.'

Giulio sits down on the bed, hunched over, suddenly looking tired and small. 'I suppose you're going to say it was only a matter of time.'

A look of contempt steals over her face. 'Now is certainly not the time for a row.' She moves towards the door, saying. 'We must be gone by dawn. You need to go over to Dante's right now, to borrow the donkey. His son is probably willing to help us for a bit of money.'

Before the cold light of dawn has arrived, the children stand in a row by the front door. They look unusually fat, for once, in layers of clothing and are uncharacteristically quiet; knowing this is serious but too afraid to ask. Vivian, pleased at her foresight last summer, slips the woollen balaclava she knitted on each of their heads, and another woolly hat on top of that. On the edge of town, the donkey stands stock still in the intense, white cold. Air condenses from his nostrils, making him a ghostly apparition in the ethereal light of the frail winter moon. Giulio, with Dante's son, finishes loading up as Vivian blows out the candle on the dresser, locks the back door, and leads the children silently down the side of the house to wait for Giulio to collect them.

Dante's son lifts Federico onto his shoulders, Giulio takes Emilio's hand and they begin their icy journey. At first, Leonardo and Emilio are excited by the adventure, but by the time they get to Maggiana, near the side track where Ma and Pa Galli live, the novelty has worn off. Leonardo calls out. 'Let's go in and surprise them.'

'Not tonight, another time,' Giulio barks, pushing him on through mud sharded with ice in order to get up to the invisibility of the woods by dawn.

Vivian puts her head down, forging on upwards, passing skeletal frozen vines with tears in her eyes as she remembers the Arcadian summers spent in that garden, amongst the fruits and flowers – a paradise lost when Mussolini declared war on England and threw in his lot with Hitler. She coughs intermittently when the biting air snaps into her lungs, while her back is bathed in a sweat. Giulio carries Emilio as much as he can, whilst Vivian pulls Leonardo along by the hand as, cold, wet and crying, they weary along the beaten track. After five unbroken hours they turn into Resinelli, forcing their way through the waist-high snow, following in a single line in the wake of the donkey whose hooves grind and crunch a way through the ice-encrusted terrain, leading them to safety.

★ ★ ★

Giovanni Farace, having arrived at the Molina barracks late the previous evening, snatches the last Populari cigarette from the packet and begins to leaf through the *Corriere del Sporte*, waiting for the knock on the door. He hears footsteps in the hall, so picks up his overcoat, pushes his oily curls into his berretto da campagna and opens the door to find blue-eyed Gunther outside. Together, they make their way down the chilly corridor into a little room strewn with maps, bits of paper, ammunition ribbons and dusty beer bottles. Giovanni throws his leather gloves down on the metal table, fingering the brass knuckleduster in his trouser pocket as he watches Gunther spread a town map out on the table. He shows Gunther the rastrellamento list and outlines the short route to Giulio Ricci's house. Once his fellow Brigate Pavoni blackshirts, Achille, Mario and Cesare, arrive, they all set off.

The troupe head towards the River Meria, turning right down Via Manzoni to the lakeside, the ominous monotony of their marching feet upsetting the quiet dawn and echoing through the empty streets. They enter Piazza Roma, passing by Café Lario where Carlo broke Giovanni's nose, their ice-cracking boots pounding the cobbles, guns resting on great-coated shoulders, until finally they come to a halt at the house on the corner.

Giovanni bangs his leather fist on the door. 'Giulio Ricci, come out – you are a traitor and a spy.' A ragged cluster of people begins to gather in the Piazza; old coats, fur hats, blankets and bits of sacking thrown over nightclothes, watching quietly.

'Italy has come knocking,' Giovanni shouts. 'Open the door now,' he demands. Silence. He kicks his steel-capped right boot repeatedly against the wood. 'It's easier if you come out now, harder for you and the family if we come in.' The house remains dark and silent.

Two men cover the back whilst Giovanni wrenches the pin out of the hand grenade with his teeth, a woman shouts 'Don't!' as he flings it at the front door, blowing it apart, splintering the air with wood, acrid smoke poisoning the piazza. He and another run inside the empty house, lifting floorboards, opening cupboards, throwing stuff around in a fruitless search. 'Bastardo,' he shouts as bullets ricochet off the cooker, smash through panes of glass and scorch the bedclothes. His fury sweeps through the house like a flame as he lifts a large mirror and cracks it against his right knee before storming out of the house, roaring 'Make no mistake, I'll find whoever tipped him off,' as he fires over the heads of the retreating onlookers.

★ ★ ★

Vivian puts herself and the children to bed while Dante's son helps Giulio get a fire going before setting off back down. Giulio crawls up into the small loft space and curls up into a ball. No sooner has he fallen into an exhausted sleep than a loud banging on the door startles them all awake. Giulio lies completely still, eyes wide open, heart thumping.

'Be quiet,' Vivian commands the children as she pulls on an old dressing gown and opens the bedroom shutters to see a column of German soldiers, standing in Indian style, further up the hill, silhouetted against the skyline. Her lips turn white and her mouth feels bone dry as she looks down at the front steps to see a German soldier, a rifle over his shoulder, standing alongside an Italian interpreter, a hat pulled down low on his brow and his face covered by a black scarf.

'Open up, we're looking for partisans.'

Despite her racing pulse she keeps a calm demeanour. 'Well, there's none here. Just me and the children.'

'We'll come in anyway – come down.'

'Alright, but are you sure?' she asks in a concerned voice. 'The children have got whooping cough, that's why we're here on our own.'

The interpreter consults the soldier. An interminable pause, then, 'Nein, danke.'

The interpreter looks up again. 'No, perhaps not.'

'Good luck in your search,' she says, her heart calming each moment as she watches them walk back up to the path to join the column and move on.

'They must have come up the main path from Lecco,' Giulio says from behind her, making her jump.

She slumps down on a chair. 'What on earth are we going to do?'

He rests his head against the door jamb, the dark bluish tinge of the incipient beard matching the shadows under his eyes. 'I can't stay here, now I'm on the list they'll come looking again.'

'Where will you go?'

'There are a number of safe houses I can go to.'

'Oh, so you'll be nice and safe, but what about us, then?'

'They're not interested in you.' He points his thumb at his chest. 'It's me they want. You'll have to stay up here.'

'What if something happens to me and the boys? Have you thought about that? Do you even care?' she says wearily.

'I'll come when I can, and you know where Alberto lives.' He looks at her anxiously. 'I must go, Farace may arrive any moment now.'

'What if they come for me if they can't get you?' she shouts at his retreating back.

'They won't,' and with those words, he is gone.

★ ★ ★

Despite the monochrome white and bitter cold, Vivian feels relieved at being up in Resinelli, out of sight and out of mind of those who would do her harm. Anyway, the house in Mandello has been temporarily boarded up, so there is no choice. The boys will have to miss school, but it doesn't matter. Things have become so anarchic that it is closed half the time anyway. It is too dangerous for them, since Mandello has become a nightmare, full of innuendo and shifty eyes in tired, pale faces. She is getting used to facing the primitive struggle for survival alone and, as she goes down the six steps into the food cellar, feels comforted knowing that there is still enough food left to get by. She moves the candle along the shelf to the pomodoro sauce that she and Francesca bottled last summer. It seems a world away since they were standing over a hot cauldron of boiling water, peeling and scalding tomato after tomato, mashing them into a pulp with a fork, adding a little salicylic acid to stop the mould and throwing in some lemony wild thyme before putting it into old wine bottles and jars. Alongside she can see the roll of salami that Francesca had passed on from a nearby farmer who had taken part in the October pig killing ritual. She thanks God for Francesca, thanks her lucky stars that such a friend lives up here all the time. Her candle passes over the dried mushrooms, the green bean and fig chutney, the olive oil and the rock of parmesan, wrapped up in several layers of sacking and tied round with a piece of string, until it reaches the saving grace – the sacks of chestnuts. Leonardo comes down to help her lift one sack up the stairs, for which he is rewarded by being allowed to roast them on the wood fire in the kitchen. Emilio has permission to help with some shelling and Federico gets a look-in once the chestnuts have been crushed into powder, mixing it together with some dewormed maize flour to make a polenta.

Vivian holds her hands out towards the fire, looking down at her chipped nails and coarsened skin, a wistful expression on her face as she recalls the days of crimson varnish and black leather gloves. This unusually cold winter seems reluctant to release its icy grip and she has begun to feel invisible, cut loose from society; just like her mother, worn down simply by the daily monotony of providing. She and the boys are frozen in time, their lives on hold, just as the Allies have frozen to a halt in the mud and snow of the Appenines, waiting for the spring thaw, desperate to begin the final push across the plain of the River Po.

It isn't until the middle of March that Giulio turns up, standing in the doorway with a milk can in one hand and a brace of different-sized small birds in another. When he smiles she sees that his top two canine teeth are missing, his untidy beard has a few flecks of grey in it, and he is thinner; a mere shadow of the gorgeous, dancing man she had fallen in love with in London.

'Long time, no see. What happened to your teeth?'

'They fell out. There's a shortage of dentists on this mountain.'

'Why are you here?'

'I'm on the way down to see Father Colazzo and thought I'd bring you these.' He swings the birds towards her.

Looking at the birds, she notices that half of them are without legs and some without wings. 'What are these?' she asks.

'Songbirds.'

'How could you?' she says, a look of disgust crossing her face.

'Old Franco taught me how; with limesticks. You make a glue out of figs, any fruit, mixed with resin, coat some branches with it in a small area of wood and there you are - stuck dead birds.'

'A forest is silent without songbirds,' she says, looking directly into his eyes.

'This is the reality of Italy today. If it moves, eat it,' he says, putting the birds down. He builds up the wood fire and places a small metal ring, with twenty small spits sticking up from it, on the table and begins slowly impaling the small birds on each spit. An aroma of burnt feathers permeates the room as he lowers them onto the flames. In silence Vivian watches the hands that once caressed her thighs pull apart the puny frames, listens to the crunching of small bones and the snapping of beaks as the mouth she once kissed rips off the tiny heads.

He leans forward, holding one of the small creatures between his thumb and forefinger, his eyes meeting hers. 'I suggest you eat one?'

A secret shiver of revulsion passes through her as she finds herself looking into the eyes of a stranger. Drawing her dirty coat around her, she turns away to go upstairs. 'I'll go and get the boys for you – they might like one.'

\* \* \*

On the 21ˢᵗ April 1945 Giulio is waiting on the edge of town, letting his boots dangle against a grey wall. It is unseasonably cold this spring, so he has his grey-green military woollen jacket done up to the very top and a black beret on at a side angle. Yesterday, Milan, and the routes to it from Lake Garda and Lake Como, were machine-gunned at low altitude by Allied planes. Today, they have entered Bologna, so it's just a matter of time before the breakthrough into the Po Valley. The Russians are closing in on Hitler's bunker in Berlin. Mass strikes are paralysing Milan and Turin and he has just heard on Radio Milano a CLN proclamation to the Germans and Fascists that they must surrender or die. Everybody knows the endgame has begun, the Fascists are on the run and the partisans are becoming ever more brazen. As he examines the pebbles in the mortar he speculates on why it is that the hit-and-run of partisan warfare suits the Italian mentality, whereas the Germans seem to need commands and solid leadership. As he lights up a cigarette, he catches a distant voice becoming clearer until the words are distinct: 'O bella ciao, bella ciao, bella ciao, ciao, ciao.' Following the sound he joins scraggy, ragged-trousered Carlo on the path at the edge of the trees and, whistling the tune together, they move on down until they reach a small, ivy-covered shed dug into the hillside.

'Here we are,' Carlo says, wrenching the door open to reveal a muddy Guzzi Normale and a rusted petrol can.

With the lingering look of a lover, Giulio examines the bike, stroking the saddle. 'Where did you get it?'

'We raided a retreating group of Germans and I chose this beauty.' Carlo picks up the can. 'And the petrol to go with it.' He looks up at Giulio. 'Have you got the address?'

Giulio nods and grabs hold of Carlo's smelly, muddied coat as the engine stutters into life and they set off down to Lecco, rifles over their shoulders, a little like old times. No hanging around under a tree watching and waiting this time; Carlo waves his left hand. 'Let's go in.' He hides the bike behind a small brick wall, crosses the road and smashes the lock with the rifle butt. Putting his shoulder against the door he shoves it in and goes through, his brutal boots crushing empty Populari cigarette packets, stamping over the faces of football players adorning the front of magazines thrown over the floor, pushing through the dirty clothes strewn all around, and into the kitchen. As Giulio goes out of the side door into the small garden filled with rubble, his eye is immediately caught by the small pile of ashes in the corner. As he digs his right boot through them, a warped but still clearly recognisable fascist symbol reveals itself, still attached to a small remnant of a black shirt. He runs back into the house, saying to Carlo. 'The bastard's flown, but let's try Mario's Trattoria – you never know.'

As he turns the corner Giulio freezes – there are already men there, men in suits, collars and ties, holding rifles, surrounding Mario on the ground – men, like him, with scores to settle. A stocky man in a flat cap swings his huge chest forward and throws a grenade into the Trattoria. The explosion buckles the door and as the windows shatter small shards of glass rain down on his coat. Papers and fragments of wood leap into the air as flames light up the dank evening and Mario gets down on his knees in the soot, holding his clasped, bleeding hands out, pleading. 'Don't shoot, don't shoot – I had no choice.' Two men lift their rifles to take aim and as Mario screams Giulio turns his eyes away from the execution scene and immediately notices a shadow slip across the wall opposite. There is a man in peasant trousers and a brown felt jacket, with a red neckerchief flapping at his throat. A man whose gait he recognises and who, briefly, meets him with a smile as he ducks out of the corner of the square. Giulio gives chase but the man has disappeared up one of the alleyways, a man who is already no longer Giovanni Farace but Antonio Bossi, the freedom fighter, on his way to Brescia to make a new life and brag about his exploits as a partisan.

* * *

On the 26th April Giulio flings open the green wooden double doors of Café Lario and stands on the threshold. Now that Farace and his type are on the run, he feels hope rising in his heart. He grabs a broom and looks at Carlo. 'No damage done. Just dirty, that's all. Let's make a fresh start.' He begins sweeping the mouse droppings, cobwebs, old cans and other debris into a corner before setting the chairs and tables in order. The belt on Carlo's clean brown woollen trousers is drawn in tightly around his thin waist, his pristine and freshly-trimmed curls shine as he vigorously rubs down the counter, chasing the odour of mould away. Now that he has shaved, Giulio can see how stretched and pale his skin is.

Carlo turns towards the shelving. 'There's some beer, surrogato coffee and grappa here still.'

'And I've got some bread and cheese, let's sit down,' Giulio replies, switching on Radio Milan. Music is playing. 'It won't be long before there's some sort of announcement. They're coming thick and fast now.'

Carlo gobbles up some bread and cheese. 'I've heard the Fascist barracks on the outskirts of Milan have been captured, shops are shuttered and German tanks were disabled on the fairground. The newspapers are in partisan hands.'

'How do you know all this?'

'Guido told me. And, he said the Germans shot political prisoners who were trying to escape from San Vittore prison.'

The music stops and a voice comes on, saying through the static that the CLN has taken power in Milan. 'Long live the Socialist Republic of Milan.'

Giulio jumps up. 'Come on, we can't just sit here. Let's go down to Como and see if Mussolini's in his Casa Fascio.' He locks up and they set off on Carlo's motorbike under the glowering sky, the lake barely visible through fine drizzle, passing a platoon of muddied, miserable Germans in retreat. Snaking their way up the road and heading north, out of Italy.

As they drive into the city in turmoil, they see Black Brigade members openly wearing red partisan bandannas around their necks and partisan units entering public buildings, tearing down Mussolini photos from walls. They learn that the prefect Celio wants an agreement with the CLN, and that all the Prefecture employees have declared themselves to be partisans. They also learn that Mussolini left Como at 4.30am that morning, moving up the western shore of the Lake, still pursuing his fantasy of a last stand in the Valtellina up by the Swiss border. The Piazza del Popolo is teeming – men with rifles and shotguns fire in the air, shake hands, kiss women, lift children on their shoulders, sing songs and shout, 'Long Live the Socialist Republic of Milan.' Carlo and Giulio sit down on the metal chairs at a café, and Giulio orders a whole bottle of grappa. He closes his eyes for a moment, thinking of her, how they held hands in Brunate, how he loved the way she thought she was *it* drinking her Campari and soda, that sunset drive in the Alfa Romeo before the children were born, in the good times before the war. 'You know, I came here once with Vivian.'

Carlo glances towards him. 'Did you. How is she?'

Giulio looks down at his boots. 'We don't talk any more.' Hearing shouting, he turns his head to see a wavy-haired man in a pale trenchcoat, his open necked shirt displaying the red neckerchief, coming towards them. His mouth is wide open as he takes a breath from the bottom of his chest and shouts, like a town crier, 'Vittoria, Vittoria – the Allies have entered Milan.' As he passes their table he grabs the grappa bottle and takes a swig before slamming it back down and disappearing into the milling crowd once more, shouting even louder 'Vittoria, Vittoria.' Giulio fills their glasses to the brim, Lifting his glass high up in his right hand he looks across at Carlo. 'Well, cheers. Here's to Vivian, then.'

★ ★ ★

On Sunday the 29th April 1945, Vivian sits down on the doorstep, resting her head against the door jamb, listening to the

single tolling bell of the Church of the Sacred Heart summoning the people of Resinelli to Mass. It sounds clear and pure, arching up into the blue sky, oblivious in its purity to all the pain and suffering of the war going on below. Solitude enhances her yearning for home and she can't even find solace in the possibility of a letter from her mother. A lonely prisoner trapped in an eyrie, she watches people answering the call to mass and envies them their capacity to pray, for the comfort it brings them. She sees Father Colazzo climb up the steps: a good man, bringing them the certainty of ritual in a time of need. Thinking of a different church, St. Giles' Church in London, a grim smile plays across her lips as she recalls those moments under the Ruskin window, remembers that desperate prayer for Giulio's forgiveness. It all seems like a million years ago to her now. But there will be no praying this time. She knows now that she will have to seek her own salvation.

No sooner has she gone inside than the sound of running footsteps getting nearer and nearer can be heard. Swivelling round as the door bursts open and crashes against the wall, she sees Francesca rushing towards her, black eyes wide open, and mouth gaping in shock. She grabs Vivian's arms with both hands, tears running down her face. 'He's dead, he's dead.'

With her heart in her mouth Vivian asks 'Who's dead?

'It's over, it's all over.'

'Is it Sergio? Is it Giulio?' She clutches at Francesca's shoulders. 'Who are you talking about?'

'Mussolini, Mussolini!'

Relief floods through her veins. 'Are you sure?'

'Yes, yes. Radio Milano says so. His body is in Piazzale Loreto, Milan, with Clara Petacci and 15 others. He was shot by partisans yesterday – near Dongo.'

Vivian, stunned, follows the agile, breathless Francesca up towards the church, where people are either talking quietly in groups or standing around with stupefied expressions on their faces. Can it be possible? Il Duce dead? The man who promised them a new Roman Empire, who harried and harangued them, energized and enchanted them, entertained them with his love-life, led them into a fatal embrace with Hitler. Can it be possible he is dead? Found hiding in a German uniform in the back of a German truck making its way, not to the last stand in the Valtellina, but to the Swiss border. Nobody seems to know what to do, and there is a palpable atmosphere of sadness in the air. Vivian notices nobody is celebrating like they did on Armistice Day. Everyone is simply too tired.

★ ★ ★

MARA G. FOX

Francesca throws a couple of newspapers down on the table in
front of her. 'It's not nice, take a look.' With revulsion Vivian
stares at the pictures of the mutilated corpse of 61 year-old
Mussolini, and his 25 year-old mistress, Clara Petacci, hanging upside down from petrol-station girders, like meat car-
casses. Neither have shoes on, and both are dressed casually,
for indoors: Mussolini in a short-sleeved shirt and Petacci in
a gabardine tailleur. The huge crowd in Piazzale Loreto had
their revenge as the bodies were kicked, spat on, urinated on
and had all kinds of rubbish thrown at them. One by one they
were strung up, Mussolini first and then Clara Petacci, as the
sun shone down on that bright spring day. She reads that a
priest had taken pity on Clara and tied her skirt up with a
piece of rope, pinning it with a clothes peg, because she didn't
have any knickers on. Also that alongside her hung some of
the most feared Fascists of the first hour – Alessandro Pavo-
lini, head of the brutal Blackshirt Brigades, and Achille Sta-
race, Secretary of the Fascist Party. Reading that Mussolini's
skull was cracked and one of his eyes fell out of its socket,
she can't bear any more and casts the newspapers aside, feeling
sick. She goes out for some fresh air and stands looking at the
Grigna mountains. Francesca follows her outside and stands
beside her.

'How could they? How could that crowd have descended
so low?' Vivian says.

'I don't know. I'm ashamed,' Francesca replies.

★ ★ ★

On the 1ˢᵗ May, Vivian learns that Radio Germany has announced the death of Hitler and despite being aware that she is living through a grand moment of history, she feels strangely numb. The horror of the war may be nearly over, but the natural optimism of spring has been disturbed and the stultifying hand of winter still has her in its grip. The frustration of inaction, the boredom of waiting has tired her out – she feels emptied, dead inside. Dumping her cup down on the table, she goes outside to find the boys engaged in snail races, and sets about finding her own snail so that she can join in. After a short time, and to her surprise, she sees Giulio arriving with a barrocino cart and horse. She manages a small smile. 'At last. I was beginning to wonder what had happened to you.'

'I've been sorting things out in Mandello,' he says, striding into the house.

She quickly follows. 'Is it safe to go down now?'

'Safe enough. Everybody's become a partisan, of course. We'll have to live with Papa. Alberto's house is too damaged.' He makes himself a small coffee and sits down, avoiding her eyes. 'We'll leave in the morning.'

Vivian moves to the window, looking out, hiding her shock at the news that she is not going home, not going back to where the children were born, and asks. 'What about our things, the furniture and the pictures?'

'We'll just have to see how much room there is.'

Realising that there isn't going to be a discussion, the unspoken fact of her total dependency hangs suspended in the air, her humiliation complete. She turns round with a blank expression. 'What's happening down there? Is anything functioning?'

'Carlo's back home. Guiseppe and Ricca are free now – their house is just dirty, not damaged.' He lights a cigarette and puts his leg up on a chair. 'I want to get the café going again as soon as possible.'

'Good, I'll go and get the boys ready then,' she says, her eyelids already swelling with the first tears as she leaves the room.

★ ★ ★

'As a result of recent measures the number of assassinations in Milan at night are going down. Last night there were 4 as against a figure of 44 on the night of May17/18. In the provinces shootings seem to be going on sporadically... Semi-legal extraordinary military Tribunals are functioning in Milan and Como and have imposed and carried out several death sentences. Procedure and organization of these courts are most unsatisfactory...'

*– Report of Sir Noel Charles, 23rd May 1945*

There is a light spring rain falling as the barrocino cart begins its descent into Mandello, and Vivian becomes increasingly aware of a strange smell in the air, a metallic rankness that sets her teeth on edge. As they pass by the stream, closer to the town, the main lakeside road becomes visible and she can see abandoned trucks, burnt-out cars, mortars and their unwanted shells, standing on the silver shining mud, and tin cans, helmets, torn rags, lying amongst the dripping bushes:

the detritus of war left behind by the retreating Germans.

The boys jump down and run quickly into the house shouting, 'Nonno, Nonno.' As Vivian reaches into the back of the cart she says to Giulio. 'Where is Papa?'

'He'll be in his room.' Giulio replies, taking a suitcase in his right hand. 'He doesn't go out now – his knees have gone.' The boys runs out into the kitchen as he opens the door to a room beside the kitchen and shouts. 'Papa, it's Vivian.'

Luigi gives her a toothless grin, revealing gums where the gold-tipped front teeth used to be. His whole body seems smaller and his left hand, full of dark age spots, has a tremor. 'It seems like yesterday,' he says.

Vivian, shocked at the difference since she last saw him, goes over and puts her hand on his shoulder. 'How are you?'

He looks at her with rheumy, exhausted eyes and smiles. 'Maria will be here soon.' Vivian looks across at Giulio with a puzzled expression.

'He gets confused now.'

Vivian looks back at Luigi. 'Oh, that'll be nice.' She moves towards Giulio, her face held rigid to avoid crying. 'Where's my room?'

'I'll show you,' he says. Her hands tremble and her nails are white as she clutches the handle of her little black suitcase and follows him up to the second floor.

After unpacking her few possessions and sorting out the boys' clothing, Vivian slips out of the back door, turning towards the lake. Passing by Villa Setmani, she notices the iron spear-topped gates have gone, the hinges empty and bare, the blue shutters are peeling, with slats missing, and nettles are beginning to forge their way up through the rusting carcass of a Kubelwagen. As she passes by several locked buildings, their boarded-up windows like sightless eyes, her pace quickens, her shoes start slipping and sliding on bits of gritty mud. Her heart is racing as she rushes towards her past, forging on down to the lake, back to the happy days. Breathless, she finally reaches Uncle Alberto's house to find the front door is planked over and the lower windows are covered in torn sacking. Vivian peers through a hole in the material at fragments of mirror lying amongst dirty rags. On the charred floorboards, broken bits of crockery jut out at bizarre angles and a dark piece of furniture crouches in the corner. She sees there is a veneer of mould over everything and, feeling queasy, recoils from the nauseating, musty smell. Sitting down on the step next to a rusting metal cooking pot, she picks a sprig of the oregano she had planted long ago, crushing it between her fingers, its sweet aroma embodying all the happiness of those early years. A terrible sadness engulfs her as she yearns for the return of those golden days. As she lowers her head onto her knees, her whole body begins to shake as sobs overwhelm her and she is consumed by tears. She knows that she will never live here again; knows all that was beautiful has been shattered, never to return.

Turning into Piazza Roma, her face all red and blotchy from crying, she hears shrieking and sees three women boxed in a corner by a group of men, their hands tied behind their backs. One is clearly a frightened teenager, her neck thrust forward, dark tresses of hair trailing towards the ground. Two men hold onto her arms as another begins shaving her head. A shrivelled old man with close-cropped grey hair, passing by, shouts out. 'Leave them alone, it's history now.' The man with the razor lifts it away from her half-shaved head and turns his callous eyes towards the old man, points the razor at him and with a vicious thrust says. 'Why, is she a friend of yours?' The old man moves on and Vivian looks at the second woman, standing upright, her bony scalp full of small tufts and bloody nicks. She has a look of quiet defiance on her face, as a man with a red scarf around his neck paints 'M' for Mussolini on her bare head. Vivian catches the eye of the third woman, a placard marked 'collaborator' hanging across her chest. With a start she recognizes her as the woman in the headscarf who spat at her in the bread queue and quickly hurries out of the Piazza; away from that bitter, defeated gaze that holds within it the sorrow of a vanquished nation.

★ ★ ★

As the days pass, Vivian finds she is used to seeing searches conducted in the street, in front of a house, outside a restaurant, behind the church. A group will surround a person, their dirty, eager hands frisking and squeezing, removing shoes, rummaging in underwear. But it's the savagery at night time that is the most difficult; lying awake, alone, listening to scurrying feet outside the window, to the sudden shots and sharp cries as someone is dragged off to face a drumhead tribunal – the perfect environment for thwarted lovers or vindictive neighbours to perjure their souls in the white heat of revenge. Every problem seems magnified by the darkness and Vivian longs for the undramatic, the solid, the grey – the land where people reach for the teapot rather than the melodrama of the gun. A longing for England that has become a constant ache.

Glad to see the livid dawn breaking against the shutters, Vivian gets up and creeps ghost-like down the stairs, letting her fingers slide down the bannisters, passing Giulio's room and that of the boys, until she reaches the kitchen. Standing in the doorway, like an intruder, she looks at the scuffed and scarred kitchen table where Maria prepared dinner and where she, as a welcome guest, ate those delicious meals. She enters and goes over to the window, looking out into fading darkness and studies the reflection of herself in a pane of glass, taking in her dishevelled hair and the shadow of middle-age clearly visible on her 34-year-old face. Not wanting to recognise herself, she looks away and, after setting out the pre-school breakfast, returns to her room to lie down. There is something pressing between her brain and skull, a weight that dulls her senses. She feels she is dying, has been slowly dying for months now. Nothing matters any more. Everything is ruined, Italy is ruined, she is ruined and she deserves to be.

★ ★ ★

Vivian heads down to the kitchen for a drink to find Carlo and Giulio sitting at the table. Carlo gets up to kiss her. 'How are you now? I hear you're not well.'

She gets a glass of water and sits down, brushing his concern away. 'I'm fine. What were you talking about?'

'Oh, the latest on the Dongo Treasure.'

'All I know is that the partisans found out that the Germans escorting Mussolini up the lake had thrown three sacks into the river, and they were recovered by two fishermen,' Vivian says, addressing her comments to Carlo, keeping her eyes averted from Giulio.

'Those sacks had in them wedding rings, medals, earrings and other jewellery. Donations by patriots to Il Duce's war effort in Ethiopia in 1935.'

Giulio joins in. 'There's other stuff too – taken from Mussolini and other Germans as they tried to get away. Gold coins, cheques, lira, Swiss Francs, French Francs, diamonds, jewel boxes, gold crucifixes; you name it, all seized in Dongo.' He sucks his lip in and taps the side of his nose. 'But guess what, it's gone missing and bodies with bullet holes in their necks keep being found up and down the lake.'

Tired of hearing conspiracy theories about who killed Mussolini, and now more about money and killings, Vivian changes the subject. 'How's the café?'

'Coming on,' Giulio replies, stretching his legs. 'Supplies are improving. We're redecorating and repairing. It'll take a while.'

Vivian, feeling agitated, suddenly stands up. 'I'm going to rest now. Ciao, Carlo.'

Lying on the bed, she begins twiddling the gold wedding ring on her finger. Just think, it could have been her gold ring in one of those sacks, if she'd been silly enough to join in the Rite of the Wedding Rings. A typical Mussolini tactic of mixing the ceremonial with the emotional, inviting the populace to marry Italy itself by exchanging their gold rings and getting a steel band in return. She feels ashamed, remembering her trip to Lecco and how she was nearly swept away by Il Duce. She recalls that the Queen was the first to make the sacrifice, and remembers seeing pictures of Rachele Mussolini donating her own wedding ring and that of her husband, Mussolini himself. If it hadn't been for Maria and Giulio telling her not to fall for such an obvious con, she might have joined the fat ladies in fur hats, the sleek-suited fascists and the poor peasants in zoccoli shoes, and done exactly that. But that's over ten years ago now, when she was young and stupid, enchanted by the idea of Italy and still in love with Giulio. She swings her legs over the side of the bed, stands up slowly, waits until the dizziness goes and then moves over to the washstand. With swift, urgent movements she rubs some soap on her wedding ring and, as there is no water in the jug, spits on it, wiggling it around until it gets over her bony knuckle joint, sliding off her finger in a rush. Putting the ring down on the bedside table, a strange feeling of relief comes over her, as though she has taken a big step of some sort. She closes her eyes as the same old questions surface again, spinning round and round in her head, sucking her down into a vortex of despair. How do you live with someone you no longer love? How can you live in a country that has broken your heart?

★ ★ ★

Feeling like a machine, Vivian goes through the daily motions of waking up, getting up, washing, dressing and eating. She waves automatically as she watches the boys go, fishing rods in hand, Leonardo and Emilio chattering and skipping ahead of Giulio and Federico, full of the optimism of childhood and thrilled at the prospect of a day out with their beloved Papa. It's time for her to begin her now habitual daily walk along the lakeside – she knows that people avoid her, calling her the mad Englishwoman. With her shoulders hunched, rubbing her hands together as she goes, she does not notice the splendour of early summer all around her, or that the fruits on the trees grow plumper each day, and the dancing light of the lake no longer dazzles her eyes. Her focus is elsewhere, directed towards finding a way out of this claustrophobic valley still bathed in its own blood, still full of people raw with anger and hungry for retribution. The borders are open now, she can go, so what's stopping her, what's the point of staying? After all, hasn't she served her purpose, given birth, brought her children through the war – at times, it seems to her, single-handed? She is useless now. But what about the boys, who are innocent in all this? How could she leave them? Surely that's such a betrayal of motherhood. Like a dog worrying a bone, her mind goes over and over leaving the boys. Practically, she can't take them with her and she has nothing to offer them back in England. They are Italian boys living in a country suffused with masculine superiority; far better they stay with their father. And anyway, isn't motherhood about wanting what's best for your child? She is not best for them, anymore. She doesn't fit in and they can do without the burden of an English mother. She feels a tightening in her chest, as though a metal cage is beginning to encircle her heart, encasing the feelings inside. She must be strong, must rediscover that strength of character, that resolution that brought her out here in the first place.

As she slowly turns around to go back, it catches her eye. She freezes, her body held rigid in suspended horror. Her previous complete self-absorption has rendered the shock more sudden and brutal. There at the edge of the lake, away from the sun, plopping up and down against the broken step of the stone jetty is the bloated, greyish-purple corpse of Luca Bonetti. He is stripped down to his underwear, his puffed up hands, with their blue fingers tied across his chest with a piece of rusty wire, fingernails torn out. There are bullet holes in the side of his face and neck, his mouth is wide open and his black eyes are gone. Part of his brain has oozed out into a halo shape, providing a gelatinous cradle for his head, and she staggers backwards, lunging over to the side of him to vomit into the sparkling waters of the lake.

★ ★ ★

Mandello-del-Lario
15th June 1946

My Dearest Mother,

I don't know if any of my last letters got through to you. Things are gradually changing for the better over here so I am hoping this one makes it. Did you write to me?

I am not feeling well these days and would like to come home for a little while to recuperate and now that the war is over it is possible to make the journey. The boys won't come with me as it would be difficult to cope with them at the moment. Giulio will look after them and maybe in the future will bring them over to see you.

There is so much to explain that it is impossible to even begin to try in a letter. All I can say with any certainty is that war changes everything and I am different now. I hope you can forgive me for leaving you.

Vivian

★ ★ ★

After Giulio has gone to work and the boys to school Vivian sets off, not to the lakeside this time but up the hill. Her step is more certain, her mood more secure now that she has decided. The martial debris littering the valley has gradually been cleared away and the great tyre gouges left by trucks are becoming hidden as nature reasserts itself, recolonising the soil. Now able to see things through the prism of hindsight, she thinks of Uncle Alberto with kindness. He was always so full of fun, generous, making her feel welcome, thinking of the children, taking difficult decisions, playing smart. He still seems almost invincible to her; the one who had kept the wolf from their door for as long as possible. He had always supported her; he will understand. She follows the outside wall along to the big wooden gate and, avoiding the fresh crop of nettles, leans across to the bell-pull. Feeling sweaty, she pats her hair down, pulls the belt of her light blue dress in tighter and wipes her hand across her emaciated chest. A dog barks somewhere, bolts slide back, a key unlocks and Alberto opens the door wide. 'Vivian. What a surprise. Come in.'

He looks different. What is left of his hair is close-shaven, his skin is loose at the throat, there are deep lines across his forehead; but he still has a lively gait. 'Let's go into the study, it's nice and cool there,' he says leading the way down a corridor. She follows him into the room, past the leather boots and horsewhip standing in the corner. The shutters are half-open and he sits down with his back to the light, behind the large oak desk, resting his hands on the top, looking at her. 'Now, what can I do for you today?'

'What a library,' she says, gazing around at the leather bound volumes on the shelves that line the room and then, noticing a painting, 'Is that your horse?'

'It was my horse. Disappeared three years ago. Eaten, I expect.' He sighs and pulls a silver cigar box towards him, opens it and removes a Toscano cigar, calling out in a loud voice as he does so, 'Sofia, bring us a Limoncello and some sbrisolonia into the study.' He pulls off the band, in the colours of the Italian flag, lights up and puffs quickly a few times to get the cigar going before releasing a cloud of smoke into the air. She takes a deep breath, savouring that sweet smell of the past. 'You look thin, Vivian.'

'I feel thin these days. I need a break, need to go home for a while.'

'Well, why don't you take a trip?'

'I'm worried about leaving the boys.'

Alberto nods his thanks as Sofia, his maid, brings in the Limoncello and cake. 'You don't need to worry. Giulio will look after them until you come back. There's plenty of women to lend a hand.'

'How are things with you, now?' she asks.

'Getting along, bit by bit. You know we are not a Communist state. The Church has backed the Christian Democrats and we've got rid of the King. What can I say to you? It takes time to rebuild a country after a war, but Moto Guzzi is still going, and so am I.' He raises his glass and they drink together. 'Now, why are you really here?'

'I'm here to ask you to keep an eye on things while I'm away.'

'Look, Giulio loves his sons. I know we've had our differences but he's family. We look after our families in Italy. You don't need to worry. Go home and get better.'

★ ★ ★

TELEGRAM

GOT YOUR LETTER.
COME HOME.
MOTHER.

Camberwell Green.
July 4 1946
London

★ ★ ★

Giulio rolls his sleeves up, puts on a stained white apron and begins mixing the cornflour starch with the flour. Things are getting easier with supplies now and Café Lario is on the slow path to recovery, but it will never be the same again – how could it be, with so much unfinished business, so many divided families, so much hurt? He places a lump of butter into the saucepan, bending his neck to watch it soften and liquefy, wondering how different it would have been if the war hadn't intervened. He shrugs his shoulders; it's no good trying to see down the path you didn't take. He weighs out the sugar and beats it into the butter before adding it to the ground almonds and hazelnuts, the brown sludge reminding him of walks along the River Thames. Maybe it would have been better not to come home – but I couldn't leave my family. Anyway, nobody could have predicted the war. He'd thought she'd be strong enough to cope. He separates the yolks from the white and stirs them in. And who'd have thought it would go on so long, that there'd be so many casualties? As he beats the egg whites until they are stiff, pictures of those early ski trips flash into his thoughts, frozen images of the lithe, laughing woman he had once loved, her skis all jumbled, lying in the snow, kissing his hands. But once the children came, she changed; wanted to do things differently. Always criticising and carping, always wanting to compromise, taking Alberto's side. At least she showed signs of caring then, signs of life. Now she doesn't talk at all, just wanders about, thin and disengaged. He folds in the salt and yeast, remembering the conversation last week when the decision was made. He can see her face, chalk-white as though the blood no longer circulated, those sunken violet eyes with the light gone out of them, as she mouths, 'We can't go on like this. I need to go home. Just for a while. To see my mother, to think.' He pours the mixture into a buttered, floured tin, just like they did when they first baked together, back in London. His hands are shaky as he puts it into the oven and goes to get the car ready.

★ ★ ★

Vivian takes the black leather suitcase down from the top of the wardrobe and opens it up, the royal blue linen interior flashing brightly in the sombre room. There isn't much, just a few clothes. She wraps a photograph of the boys in white hats going fishing inside the seared Italian flag Giulio brought home the night Mussolini fell, and puts her 'Teach-Your-self-Italian' book into the suitcase beside it. She reaches across the bed to pick up the Baedeker. Holding it close to her heart, she smiles bitterly at the memory of her former self, at the hopeful naïvety of her youth, and places it gently inside the suitcase and closes the lid.

It's time to go, and the boys come forward, one by one, for a kiss. She leans over, the metal cage round her heart firmly locked, and kisses each one on the forehead. 'I won't be gone for long – Papa will look after you, so be good.' She meets their eyes. 'Promise me.'

They all look at her – so pale and remote now, but still their mother, still the one they love and long to be kissed and held by – and they promise. Emilio cries. Federico clings to the folds of her skirt, but Leonardo prises his brother's fingers away and she walks out to the car.

The fountains are no longer playing as they enter the front portico of Milano Centrale Station and beggars and hawkers accost them as they enter the busy main hall. Whistles scream and dogs bark as families throw themselves into each others' arms in farewell or the enthusiasm of arrival. A small child licks her ice-cream as she waits for a train to come in, unaware of it dripping onto her shiny shoe. Vivian shows her suitcase to the haggard guard, who stabs a label marked London-Victoria via Zurich-Basel-Strasbourg-Hirson-Lille-Calais-Dover on it and they make their way along Platform 3. After helping her up the large step into the carriage, Giulio puts the little black suitcase into the overhead netting as Vivian sits down next to the window. After fumbling with a small brown bag, he removes a silver wrapped parcel and puts it on her knees. 'This is for you, a Torta Grigna, for the journey.' He looks into her face but she stares vacantly ahead. As he leaves he looks back. 'Write to me when you are ready to come home, then.'

'Thank you. I will. Perhaps in the autumn, after Resinelli.'

Aware that the guard has begun walking up the platform, closing the carriage doors, she allows herself to look at him, leaning against the same studded pillar he leant against when she arrived. He lights a cigarette and gazes at her with wistful eyes, but she feels nothing. The wheels begin to turn and squeal like a tortured animal. Chains groan and she raises her frail hand, briefly, as the train begins shuddering and jolting over the joints of the rails, out past the brick wall, on through the signals and out of sight.

Vivian knows she will never return.

## Bibliography and sources of quotations used:

Many thanks to Professor Jonathan Steinberg for his English translations of Italian texts in this novel, and his assistance with the use of these.

- Benito Mussolini, 'The Bologna Fascist Speech', April 1921. Translated by Jonathan Steinberg from his book *Deutsche Italiener und Juden Der Italiensche Widerstand gegen den Holocaust.* (Gottingen: Steidl Verlag. 1992), p.239.
- Filippo Tommaso Marinetti, *The Futurist Manifesto*, February 1909 and *Manifesto of Futurist Cooking*, August 1930. Translated by Jonathan Steinberg.
- Benito Mussolini, *La dottrina del Fascismo: I. Idee fondamentali – II. Dottrina politica e sociale,* June 1932. Translated by Jonathan Steinberg.
- Benito Mussolini, speech on Ethiopia. Recorded by LUCE in Italy on 2nd October 1935.
- Benito Mussolini, speech declaring war on England and France on 10th June 1940. Recorded by LUCE in Italy.
- Winston Churchill, shortwave radio broadcast from UK, Cairo and Athens to the Italian People on 23rd December 1940.
- Winston Churchill, speech of 27th July. Found at: http://hansard.millbank systems.com/commons. 1943/jul27/Italy-and-the-war; covered by Open Parliament Licence V.3.0.Page 111.
- Marshall Pietro Badoglio, EIAR Italian Radio Broadcast 8th September, 1943. Translated by Jonathan

Steinberg.

· Other quotes from the following War Office documents containing public sector information licensed under the Open Government Licence V.3.0. Please see www.nationalarchives.gov.uk/doc/open-government-licence/version/3/.

TNA WO 204/7283

TNA WO235/375

TNA WO204/7283

TNA W02355/375

TNA W0106/3965A

Regarding the visit to the theatre in Milan I have relied on the account by Cicely Hamilton of her own visit to the theatre to be found in *Modern Italy as Seen by an Englishwoman*. (J.M. Dent & Sons Ltd., 1932).

I would also wish to point out that I have relied on *Italy at War* by Henry Adams and the Editors of Time-Life Books (Time-Life Books Inc., 1982) and *The Last Days of Mussolini* by Ray Moseley for contextual background.

**Glossary and explanatory notes:**

*Ammassi*: storage centres for agricultural products whereby farmers had to contribute a proportion of their produce.

*Autarky*: a programme Mussolini followed to try and make Italy self-sustaining in industry and food production, the latter being called the 'Battle for Grain'.

*Avanguardisti*: a section of the Ballilla for boys aged 14 to 18 years.

*Ballilla*: 'Opera Nazionale Ballilla' (ONB). An Italian Fascist youth organisation used as an adjunct to school.

*CLN*: 'Comitato de Liberazione Nazionale'. A political umbrella organization representing Italian partisans fighting German occupation of Italy, composed of different parties all of whom were anti-Fascist.

*Dopolavoro*: The Opera Nazionale Dopolavoro was an organisation created for adult leisure and recreational purposes. In 1927 it became a subsidiary of the Fascist Party.

*Figli della Lupa*: 'children of the she-wolf'. A section of the Ballila for boys aged 6 to 8 years.

*OVRA*: 'Organizzazione per la Vigilanza e la Repressione dell'Antifascismo'. Secret police service set up in 1927 by Fascist Party to monitor and prevent anti-Fascist activity.

*Perfide Albione*: Anglophobic phrase meaning 'treacherous England'. Used by Italian Fascists to criticise the British Empire.

*Rastrallemento*: round-up or area search conducted by Germans and/or Fascists in order to arrest or kill their enemies.

*SOE*: 'Special Operations Executive'. British World War II organisation involved in espionage and sabotage in respect of Axis powers who acted in support of resistance movements.

**Italian songs quoted:**

'Bandiera Rossa'. Song associated with socialist/communist movements.

'Giovenezza'. Became known as the unofficial anthem of Italy between 1924-1943. There are different versions and

the chorus from the 1922 version is only used here.
Wikipedia has a useful outline of its development. It can
be listened to on Youtube.

'Me Ne Frego'. Used by Gabriele D'Annunzio at Fiume
and later adopted as a motto by Fascism.

'O Bella Ciao'. Based on a folk song, this was popular
with resistance movement in 1943-45. There are many
international versions of it.

## List of photographs (in order of appearance):

1. *FIAT La nuova Balilla – per tutti, eleganza della Signora.*
   'The new Fiat' Balilla, Dudovich, Marcello (1878-
   1962). Credit: De Agostini Picture Library/Bridgeman
   Images. License granted by DACS.

2. *Baedeker's Northern Italy.* Photograph by the author.

3. Pagani's Restaurant, Great Portland Street as found on
   Wikipedia.org (T138). Reproduction by permission of
   Westminster City Archives.

4. Ruskin Window, St Giles' Church, Camberwell Green.
   Photograph by the author, with thanks to St Giles
   Church for permission to use this image.

5. 'Doll drill' and 'Giovane saluting' first published in the
   book *Modern Italy as Seen by an Englishwoman* by Cicely
   Hamiton (Orion Publishing Group). Disclaimer: all at-
   tempts to trace the copyright holder were unsuccessful;
   Eyewear is proceeding to print these images with the
   original publisher's knowledge.

6. Moto Guzzi Normale, with permission of Piaggio.

7. 'Figli della Lupa.' 'Young boys and girls who are mem-

bers of the Wolf Club posing for a picture in uniform.'
(Photo by Thomas D. Mcavoy/The LIFE Picture Col-
lection/Getty Images).

8. Church of the Sacred Heart and the Grigna Mountains, Resinelli. Photograph by the author.

9. Vivian's suitcase label. Photograph by the author.